I FIGURED TO DIE QUIETLY
AS SOON AS WE SAW THE KLAN
COMING THROUGH THE TREES.

A white shape like a ghost slipped out of the woods near the tree, then another one and another. I could hardly breathe, and they were so near I could have touched them on their feet. There were six of them. They were all white except for black holes where their eyes would have been. They had no eyes, no nose, no mouth or anything. They looked like something evil from hell.

I heard a long whistle. It must have been an all-clear signal, because one of them brought out a small lantern and lit it. In the light they looked more scary than in the dark. They sure looked like they were imps of hell with a reddish glow over the black eye holes.

A little of my fear and stiffness left my body when one of them spoke, for it made them seem more human. The leader's voice was muffled as he held the lantern up high. "One of you boys shinny up the tree and look." One of the figures, smaller than the rest, climbed the tree. The other held the lantern up to the hole in the rotten tree and peered down. "Hell fire," he snapped, "there ain't no body in here."

Robbie Branscum
Me and Jim Luke

AVON
PUBLISHERS OF BARD, CAMELOT, DISCUS, EQUINOX AND FLARE BOOKS

AVON BOOKS
A division of
The Hearst Corporation
959 Eighth Avenue
New York, New York 10019

Copyright © 1971 by Robbie Branscum.
Published by arrangement with Doubleday and Company, Inc.
Library of Congress Catalog Card Number: 74-144252.

ISBN: 0-380-00354-6

First Avon Printing, June, 1975.

AVON TRADEMARK REG. U.S. PAT. OFF. AND
FOREIGN COUNTRIES, REGISTERED TRADEMARK—
MARCA REGISTRADA, HECHO EN CHICAGO, U.S.A.

Printed in the U.S.A.

Me and Jim Luke

CHAPTER 1

I knew the hand was dead the minute it touched my naked shoulder next to my overall strap. I couldn't have moved if my life depended on it, and I reckoned it did. I sort of froze, and at the same time I felt like messing all over myself. I tried to holler, but no matter how wide I got my mouth open no sound came out. I could see the light of the lantern Jim Luke carried get further and further away, and finally it was plumb out of sight. The moon was plenty bright enough to see by, but Lord I didn't want to see the thing that had hold of me. I knew if I did, I would die for sure.

Once I heard Grandpa and Grandma talking, and they said that when a body passed on, ther lives passed before their eyes. It didn't seem fair in my case because the good Lord hadn't given me much time to pass before me. But again, in my case, I'd rather think about what little living I had done than the dying I was going to do shortly, from stark raving fear.

I tried to think as long as I could, to stretch out my dying. All I could remember was not being able to remember my pa. I remembered living with my ma in town and about her telling me she had to go to a city to work because we didn't have any money, and telling me I would have to live with my grandparents on Pa's side of the family until she made a home and sent for me. I sure missed her a lot then, and still did at times, but Grandpa and Grandma lived on a small, dirt farm way back in the Arkansas hills. It was interesting. Then, too, there was Jim Luke.

When I first came to live with them, Jim Luke was ten and I was eight. Now two years had passed, but I wouldn't have bet a dime when I first came to live with them that I would live to be ten. Jim Luke had been birthed to Grandpa and Grandma after their other youngins had grown up, married and moved away. And being the only one left, that Jim Luke was hound-dog mean. He nearly knocked my head right off my shoulders the first time I called him "Uncle Jim Luke." For a long time after that I didn't call him anything. Of course, he didn't hit me around Grandpa or Grandma, but when we got out of sight of them I had to run for my life. He made me chop his share of the stovewood and do his chores around the barn until one day, about six months after I came to live with them, I got tired of the way he was doing me and fought him down by the pond until he nearly killed me. But he liked me after that and did his own work, especially after I told Grandpa that I was so beat up and bloody from falling off the bluff by the spring. From then on he called me Sammy John instead of "Hey, you," and I called him Jim Luke.

Grandpa and Grandma treated me good. But truth to tell, Jim Luke caused most of the trouble we had, and it was his fault that the dead thing had hold of me because the day before, when I got kind of sad and missed my ma he said, "Cheer up, Sammy John, iffen the moon's high I'll show ye how to possum hunt tomorrer night." Of course I perked right up because I was a fool for wanting to hunt possums.

The time was sure right for possum hunting. It was fall, with first frost making the orange and brown leaves crisp and the persimmons ploppy and sweet. Possums were crazy about persimmons, and the farm woods were thick with persimmon trees. Me and Jim Luke hogged our supper and hurried through the chores and I called Jim Luke's hound dog, Pepper, and my own hound dog, old Salt. We had named them Salt and Pepper because

Jim Luke's was black and spotted and mine was one of his pups, a dirty white. After Jim Luke lighted the lantern he stole some of Grandpa's plug tobacco and some brown sack paper so we could smoke around the campfire. I could just about taste that baked possum with red pepper, sage and sweet potatoes.

We hadn't gone two miles down the wooded path when old Salt had come sniffing and whining around the old, rotten, hollow tree. Well, old Salt had let out a wail and slunk off, and when I turned to look after him, leaning my back against the old tree, that's when that thing grabbed me, and that darned old dog just left me there. Lordy, Lordy, I sure hated to die shivering and shaking and wanting to wet my britches. My whole body was colder than the hand on my shoulder. My mouth felt full of cotton. I tried to swallow a time or two, but it felt like my Adam's apple was stuck.

Just as I was getting set to pass on as manly as I could, I heard Jim Luke calling me. After what seemed like a year and three days, I could see the light coming back, getting stronger and stronger. Jim Luke was yelling, "Sammy John, dang your hide. You'd better quit a hidin' and answer me afore I tan your dad-blamed hide."

Lord, I was trying to say something so bad I felt like it was tearing my tonsils out. I was also promising the good Lord just almost anything if he would let me holler, like how I wouldn't cuss any more. Nobody could have been more flabbergasted than me when I screamed, "Jim Luke, come get this damn thing off'n me."

Jim Luke came running with old Pepper, and I reckon it was a weird sight that met his eyes when he held the light up. I was leaning and slobbering against the old tree, and the hand was on my shoulder like the tree had sprouted it there. Of course, old Pepper let out a howl and headed for home, and Jim Luke kept running a little way after him then coming back. Me, I finally wet down my britches leg and sort of moaned, afraid he was going to lose his head and leave me there.

11

I couldn't stand it any longer and I started blubbering, "Please, Jim Luke, get this thing off'n me. Iffen ye do, I'll give ye anythin' I got that ye want. Please, Jim Luke.

"Aw hell, Sammy John," he said, "ya don't think I'd leave ya here, even a no-good boy like you."

At his words I quit crying, as I knew Jim Luke would do what he said.

He put the lantern down and hunted around until he found an old stick, then nearly whopped me to death trying to knock the hand off me without getting any closer to it himself. But I wasn't complaining any because I'd rather have been beaten to death any old time by Jim Luke than to be scared to death with that old dead hand.

Finally I was plumb past feeling, and don't really remember just when Jim Luke got the hand off me and pulled me clear with one hand and held the lantern with his other hand while running with me. Man I tell you, that Jim Luke can run.

We were nearly home when Jim Luke, panting like a dog, stopped and sat on a log and made me sit beside him. My rear end was sitting, but my feet were still running. He rolled us some cigarettes with Grandpa's plug tobacco in strips from the brown sack paper, and after a few drags I forgot all about the dead hand and started puking. My head was going around on my shoulders and my belly was trying to crawl out of my throat. The world was whirling around and the moon was spinning. The trees and Jim Luke looked deader than anything I had ever seen. He was just holding onto the log and was kind of green, but not puking like me.

The lantern went out, and leaving it there we sort of crawled up the path to the house. Grandpa and Grandma were already in bed, so we slipped into ours and held on when it started to spin. Lord, it seemed like the end of the world, like nothing would ever be the same again.

It must have been nearly daylight when I found that if

12

I opened my eyes and stared straight up at the ceiling things didn't spin so bad. Jim Luke was snoring and moaning once in a while. I was sort of cold, and wished I had taken off my wet overalls. I hoped Jim Luke hadn't seen them or when he got mad at me he would holler, "Baby, baby, pee'd your britches."

Familiar sounds seeped into my tired ears, soothing them. I could hear old Ned stomping restlessly in the barn stall. That old mule was more stubborn than Jim Luke. Once in a while the chickens in the chicken house fluttered their wings, and before long, Charley, the rooster, would crow sunup. I could hear Bessy, the fattening sow, grunt as she turned her heavy body over. I got to wishing Jim Luke would quit naming our winter meat "Bessy," because after butchering time when I asked Grandma for something to eat, she would say, "Go get a piece of old Bessy's side meat in a biscuit," or "There's still some of Bessy's liver left." It just sort of took my appetite away. I felt better about eating things that didn't have any name, but it didn't bother Jim Luke. He was always saying at breakfast, "Pass me some of them eggs and old Bessy." It just about made me throw up, but Grandma and Grandpa didn't seem to mind.

Jim Luke didn't look like Grandpa or Grandma at all. Grandma was short and fat with big round blue eyes and white hair wrapped around and around her head in fat braids. Grandpa was tall, dark and slim with black hair and bright blue eyes. I looked a lot more like him than Jim Luke did, except I was short and my eyes were nearly as black as my hair. Jim Luke was tall and it seemed like his body was mostly long, skinny arms and legs. He had a big head covered with straw-colored hair. He had big teeth, and the biggest ears I had ever seen. His face was covered with big brown freckles, and his eyes were slanted and green like Tom Jones, our old tomcat.

It was funny that I had ever thought of them as strange or the farmhouse either, now I liked them and the house. The house had four rooms; two bedrooms, one for Grandpa and Grandma and one for me and Jim Luke. The furniture consisted of iron bedsteads covered with bright quilts that Grandma had made herself. There was a great big kitchen that held a huge black wood cookstove. The stove had a warming oven where Grandma kept the leftover food. There was also a big table with benches to sit on, and there were shelves in the corner for dishes. We had a back porch where a well was to draw our water from, with a stand near it for a water bucket, a gourd dipper, wash pan and a dish to hold Grandma's lye soap. The front room also had an iron bedstead for company to sleep on, or on which to lay babies when aunts came to visit. It also held a pot-bellied heating stove and a wood box, a dresser where a body could see half of himself at a time, and a whole bunch of rocking chairs. We had a big front porch, too, where we sat in the summer after it got dark. Grandpa and Grandma would rock and tell me and Jim Luke about when they were young, while we dangled our feet off the porch and watched lightning bugs glowing in the dark like millions of tiny lanterns.

Lanterns! Oh my, Lordy, Lordy. We forgot the lantern and would have to go back near the tree with the dead hand. If we lost that lantern Grandpa would skin us alive. Charley started to crow, the bed stopped swaying. I tried to rouse myself and think of how we could get the lantern without going back close to that tree. But it was too much, I had to sleep.

CHAPTER 2

I woke up with Jim Luke nearly shaking my head off. For a minute I thought I was going to be sick again. "Quit it!" I yelled. "Stop a shakin' me. Turn me loose."

"All right," Jim Luke hissed in my ear, "but listen, Sammy John, don't ye say a word to Pa and Ma. Ya hear?"

"About what?" I yelped, then remembered and started shaking on my own accord. "I won't tell, Jim Luke, but Lordy, what're we gonna do? I mean somebody's gotta know."

"Listen, Sammy, I been thinkin' for an hour whilst you been snorin'," Jim Luke whispered, leaning over me with his green eyes slitted and gleaming, "Well, there might be a reward for that dead man and the killer too. Why, iffen we find out who killed him we could get a lot of money and you could send fer your ma, and I could get that double-barreled shotgun from the catalogue, and maybe some real race horses 'stead o' ridin' old Ned. Now don't tell till we can find the killer. Okay, Sammy John?"

The thoughts of all that money made the greed in me float up to the surface, and I knew my eyes were gleaming as much as Jim Luke's, but I was slighty worried. I said, "But Jim Luke, how in cat hair are we gonna find who killed him? I mean somebody coulda brought him from fer away, like town or someplace."

"Nah, ain't no chance, Sammy John," Jim Luke whispered. "Now listen, somebody around here had to a done it, fer nobody away from here woulda knowed about that old tree and that it was holler. As soon as we can get away, we'll go take a look at him and poke his hand back in that tree afore somebody spots 'im."

I sure didn't cotton to the idea that one of our neighbors was a killer, and worse still I didn't like the idea of going back to that tree. But before I could get over it again, Grandma called us. We rushed out to the kitchen just as she was pulling an old black bread pan full of brown biscuits from the oven. We washed at the stand by the well. Lordy, that water was so cold it took all the sleepy tiredness out of us.

After we were all at the table with our plates filled, Grandpa grinned at us, "Well, are we gonna eat possums and sweet taters tonight?"

"No luck, Grandpa," I said quick as I could, but Jim Luke's sharp elbow nearly took the breath out of me, and he jumped in with, "Pa, we didn't catch no possums last night, but boy did we ever run into what looked like the dad-blamedest nest of old granddaddy gray squirrels ya ever did see. And Pa, we want to go back today and mark the place, and Ma, we'll be eatin' fried squirrels all winter. We left the lantern to mark the place." He ran to a stop and gave Grandpa a slant-eyed look to see how it was going over.

My heart fell and I felt kind of glad at the same time when Grandpa said, "Well now, I don't know about that, boys. Ya know we gotta finish stockin' the feed in the north forty 'cause winter's nigh on us and the cattle's gotta eat. 'Sides that, school'll be startin' afore long and we gotta get it all done while we can."

"Shoot fire," Jim Luke swore under his breath. I sneaked a look to see if Grandpa or Grandma heard him, but if they did they acted like they didn't. They knew that Jim Luke was a devil to whop, though Grandpa laid it on him sometimes, but mostly it was just easier to act like a person didn't hear or see what he did.

Grandpa went on, "So when you boys get the feedin'

16

done, harness old Ned to the wagon and get the knives sharpened. Maybe iffen we go at it hard, we'll be through by noon, 'cause I shore don't want to leave that lantern, and you boys'll have time to get out and mark that squirrel's den."

A body would have thought that would perk Jim Luke up, but he cussed steadily from the time he took a last swipe at the gravy on his plate straight through sharpening the knives while I turned the old grindstone, and until we had old Ned and the wagon ready to go. I didn't say much, I had learned long ago to let Jim Luke get all cussed out by himself. I guess he felt like Grandpa was holding that huge pile of reward money out from under this nose.

I liked to bounce around on the wagon seat, holding the long sharp knives careful like, with Grandpa hawing and geeing at the mule. The sun rose warmer and warmer. The air smelled good, birds sung and squirrels chattered. Holly berries dripped red against the greenness of the trees, and oak and blackgum trees showed brown and orange leaves. Acorns fell with every breeze. The barely open trail looked like we were the first settlers over it. It was fun to pretend there were Indian warriors lurking behind the trees, and pretty soon we would have to pull our wagons in a circle and defend our lives. Even Jim Luke's muttered curses in the background were a part of the peaceful scene.

We were nearly to the cornfield when we came to the pond in the middle of the trail. It had been a dip, but Grandpa had dammed up both ends so it would hold water. He always drove the wagon across, and when we got in the middle he would stop and let old Ned drink and rest a little. Then Jim Luke would always stand up on the tail gate and pee out in the water as far as he could. There wasn't much life in the water except for frogs and mosquitoes, but Grandpa didn't like for Jim Luke to pee in it. Jim Luke always laughed and said that he reckoned he would give the frogs warts for a change.

17

I could hear old Ned slurping water and Jim Luke peeing, but my mind was on the Indian chief behind the sycamore. I could just see the tip of his feathered headdress, and had a good bead on him with my imaginary gun when Grandpa scared the britches nearly clean off me by suddenly yelling, "Hey, up there," and whacked old Ned across the back with the reins, sending him suddenly humping up the bank, quickly jerking the wagon after him. I heard a curse and a splash in back of me, and when Grandpa had stopped old Ned I looked back and saw Jim Luke sitting in the pond wide eyed and white looking. Then he turned red. Dripping and steadily cussing again, he heaved himself out of the pond and walked toward the cornfield, not even looking at us. Grandpa laughed to himself as we rode on.

The cornstalks were dry and rustling, and smelled clean and sunshiny. Grandpa tied the reins to the wagon and old Ned clomped close beside us, dragging the wagon slowly and eating bits and pieces of the fodder as we cut the stalks with our knives. When we had an armful we threw it in the wagon. Nobody talked, and Jim Luke stayed way ahead of me and Grandpa. I don't know whether it was to hurry and keep warm or to get the field finished quickly so we could go and find the killer and get all that money, or because he was still mad at Grandpa for making him fall in the pond. I wasn't in much of a hurry, for the dead hand the night before seemed more like a dream than a reality. But it didn't keep me from wondering which one of our neighbors had done it. We sure had some odd ones around; still there wasn't any of them I didn't like.

We still didn't have the cornstalks cut at noon, so Grandpa brought out some biscuits that Grandma had filled with last year's old Bessy. Judging by the frost the night before, it wouldn't be long until it was time to kill this year's. There were some green onions from the garden in the basket, and a jar of lukewarm buttermilk. All in all it was pretty good eating, and even Jim Luke sat with us, so I figured he wasn't mad any more. We swallowed as fast as we could, not talking, because we wanted to hurry and get through. No matter how fast we worked though it was still midafternoon when we got through. Grandpa drove old Ned as fast as he would go to get home. There weren't any Indians hiding behind the trees for me this time; it was more like dead men, and I kept my eyes straight ahead.

When we got to the barn Grandpa unloaded the wagonload of fodder into the corncrib while Jim Luke and I fed and watered the stock, fed the chickens, gathered the eggs and slopped old Bessy. Grandpa always did the milking, so we didn't have to worry about that. Old Pepper and Salt kept leaping around us, but Jim Luke ran them off. We didn't want them following us, at least Jim Luke didn't, but I would just as soon have had all the company we could get.

As soon as we finished, we hollered to Grandpa that we were going to get the lantern and mark the squirrel nest. First we detoured through the kitchen. There was a pan of fried potatoes on the stove, a pot of pinto beans and a pan of corn bread. Grandma wasn't to be seen, so we cut all the corners from the bread and slit them, then filled the slits with fried potatoes. Just before we ducked out of the door to keep Grandma from catching us, Jim Luke sneaked and opened the corner cabinet and poured some of Grandpa's homemade medicine into an empty fruit jar of Grandma's. Grandpa would have had a cat fit for sure if he had caught us, so we ran until we were out of sight of the house, then slowed to a walk, cramming the bread and potatoes down our throats. At every step I was complaining to beat the band, "Jim Luke, you know dang good and well Grandpa'll take the hide off'n us when he misses his medicine. You know how he allus told us not to tech it."

"Oh shut your dad-blamed mouth, Sammy John," he snapped, "you know damn good and well it ain't nothin' but plain old moonshine. They ain't no need to be polite about it just 'cause Pa is, and 'sides a good slug o' this'll stop you from shakin' and peein' on yourself when we

19

put the hand back and look for clues. And 'sides," he laughed shyly, "this stuff of our'n is strong enough even to make the arm of the dead man come alive."

That shut me up for sure. If there is anything I am more afraid of than a dead man, it's a live dead man. So when Jim Luke swallowed a big drink from the jar when we were close to the tree, I did the same. We had to hold on to each other for a while to keep the stuff from knocking us off of our feet. Even while we were hugging, a deep warm glow flowed up from my toes to the top of my head. We turned each other loose and started grinning like fools for just no reason at all. It was a beautiful night suddenly, and I was the bravest of the brave. Jim Luke and I were the greatest detectives living, and we had a job to do, a killer to find, justice to render, and before five minutes had passed we had taken another slug from the jar and were drunker than hoot owls, but brave.

I didn't even hesitate when we got to the rotten tree, but went straight at it to look the hand over. Even with the whiskey inside me I nearly got sick, because the hand was swollen and black, and I didn't want to touch it. It hung from a slit in the hollow tree. The tree was broken off about ten feet above the ground, and Jim Luke said he figured it had taken a mighty tall person to poke the body down into it. I had to admire Jim Luke, he poked the dead hand back through the slit in the tree and stopped the slit with bark, and didn't show a flicker of sickness or anything else on his face; but he did take a big slug of whiskey right away. I turned it down when he passed it to me. It was Jim Luke who climbed up the tree and peered down to see if we knew the dead man. I was shaking some because Jim Luke stared down that tree for a long time, but he shook his head when he stepped back on the ground.

"Aw Sammy, he ain't nobody we know. I can't rightly tell what he looks like, but he's got red hair and he's wearin' store-bought clothes. Man, ain't nobody around here has red hair and wears store clothes. Shore wish we could look in his pockets, but I'm afeared we'd break the tree more than 'tis, so we got to spy around and find out what secrets our neighbors have got to hide."

"I don't like it, Jim Luke. They might kill us too." I half expected any minute for somebody to step around a tree, pointing a gun at us.

"Naw." he said, "nobody'd suspect us anyhow, They'd think we were too little to find anything out, 'sides nobody knows we found him." He led the way back to the log where we left the lantern the night before.

When we sat down on the log, Jim Luke reached for the tobacco and papers he had left there, but when he offered them to me I shook my head and he put them in a hole in the log to save for when we came to look at "our body" again.

Jim Luke passed the fruit jar again and I took a few big swallows. He drank the rest of it and said, "Sammy, I reckon we better get goin' iffen we're gonna spy on folks tonight."

My tongue felt heavy and thick. I tried to say that Grandpa and Grandma wouldn't let us out late, and I guess it came out clear enough because Jim Luke said, "They won't know nothin' about it iffen we wait till they're asleep and climb out a winder, and come back afore sunup."

I don't know why I said I was all for it, but it sounded like a grand, exciting thing for two great detectives to do.

When we got up off the log, the world rose with us. In fact, the hill toward the house got so steep we had to climb it on our hands and knees. I wanted to tell Jim Luke how strange it was for the hill to suddenly raise up, but it took all I could do to keep climbing, and I was afraid that if I turned loose with my hands I would fall back to the bottom.

When Jim Luke and I got to the top of the hill, the world had settled some and I was sure surprised to see that we were crawling. Jim Luke had the lantern handle between his teeth so his hands would be free for climbing. I kept trying to tell him how funny it was that we had to climb up a hill that was nearly level, when Jim Luke poked me and pointed toward the house. Lord have mercy, there came Grandpa with a long switch. So, he had missed his medicine after all.

"Sammy John," Jim Luke hissed, "we're gonna get it for sure, so you scream a lot and he'll quit sooner. Hear me? You holler!"

Grandpa stopped right in front of us and stared for a while, and without a word he stepped behind Jim Luke and brought down the switch, whop. Jim Luke's mouth opened and the lantern dropped. I thought my ears would burst with his "Shoot fire! Oh hell, Pa. Shoot fire!"

I barely remember getting hit. I was more concerned right then with my belly than with my hind end, and the switch was just an added pest. I started puking my head off and my guts out, and I didn't care if Grandpa beat me to death. In a way I wished he would, and hurry about it before I turned myself plumb inside out. Somewhere about that time I quit remembering anything at all and didn't know anything until I half came to in the bed in the middle of the night.

Jim Luke was laying on his belly and still saying, "Shoot fire!," so I just went to sleep again, though not before I told myself that no matter what Jim Luke said I wasn't going to smoke any more or take any more of Grandpa's medicine.

CHAPTER 3

The next morning I felt my tongue had grown on to the roof of my mouth, and my head hurt something powerful. I must have drunk a bucket of water. Jim Luke was pale and not talking, and neither was Grandpa or Grandma. I didn't have anything to say either, and the sight of old Bessy laying on a platter next to the eggs made me sicker than ever. But one blessed thing, Grandma didn't keep saying for us to eat as she almost always did. For some unexplained reason, Grandpa kept having fits of laughing all day.

Me and Jim Luke just about half did what work we were supposed to do that day, and either sat with our feet hanging off the front porch or sat next to the well and took turns drawing up cool buckets of water to drink. Sometimes we just laid on the porch with old Salt and Pepper and rubbed their bellies or picked ticks off them. I don't remember ever feeling so miserable in my whole life. At about time for the sun to set I got to feeling better and so did Jim Luke, except he still favored his rear end when he sat. When Grandma's supper-cooking smell came floating out the window, I felt hungry for the first time that day, and I saw Jim Luke's Adam's apple bob up and down as he swallowed, and though he said nothing, I knew he was hungry too. Jim Luke didn't talk much any time, but even less after he had a whopping. I suspect he held grudges for a spell.

Grandpa was still having fits of laughter over nothing

23

at all when Grandma called us to supper, but even that was past being strange. A body could only take so much, and after all my mind had been through the last two days, I was beginning to be sort of numb and shock proof. I felt tired and sleepy after putting away a batch of potatoes and beans, so without a word or waiting for Jim Luke, I went to bed before good dark.

I was dreaming that the dead hand had hold of me. I was twisting and turning, trying to get away when I came fully awake with Jim Luke nearly shaking my head off and hissing in my ear, "Sammy John, Sammy John. Iffen you want half of that reward money you'd better wake up and help me spy. Ya hear?"

"I hear ya. Turn me loose. And ya better give me half the money, 'cause it was me that the hand caught. Hey, who are we gonna spy on?"

"Ole Zack," Jim Luke hissed. "Hurry and get your britches on, and don't make no noise." Jim Luke raised the window quiet like while I pulled on my britches, then we slipped through it.

The moon was almost as bright as day, and the fallen leaves were cold and crunchy with frost on my bare feet. I stood on one foot and then the other while we listened to see if Grandpa or Grandma had heard us. Hearing no noise, we stepped through the back yard and went down by the barn, stopping to pee against the chicken house. Then we cut through the orchard and took a little-used path through the west pasture. It was dark under the trees, but with bright lacy spots where the moon shone through.

It was about four miles to old Zack's place, and we never went there much. Everybody, including me and Jim Luke, thought he was a little touched because he had about a dozen brooder hens and two skinny roosters, and he had a strange fixation that somebody was going to steal them. He spent most of his nights creeping around the chicken house with his shotgun and Sam Smith, his hound dog. That was odd in itself, because we had never heard of a body naming an old hound dog two names.

When we got to the rickety, falling down fence that surrounded the farm, we dropped to our bellies and crawled until we were within twenty-five yards of the house. Everything stood clear and white in the moonlight. Zack's house was leaning sideways and the porch roof sagged in the middle. It looked like a big puff of wind would blow it over. But his chicken house was strong and painted white. It looked brand new against the old faded grayness of the house.

I strained my eyes and could see nothing. I was afraid my toes were going to drop off from frost-bite by the time Jim Luke poked me in the ribs. Then I clamped a hand over my mouth to make sure I wouldn't yell out loud, which was a good thing, for the last few days had sure made me spooky. I tried to focus my eyes on the spot where his finger was pointing, and there, plain as day, was old Zack creeping around the chicken house on his hands and knees, holding his shotgun. All he had on was his long-handled drawers and a pair of boots. The flap of the underwear was down, lifting a little as the breezes blew, and Sam Smith crept not far from Zack's old, naked hind end.

He was crawling around the corner of the chicken house away from us when we saw Sam Smith stumble and run his cold nose up old Zack's naked hind end. Old Zack rose up with a howl and swung around to see what had hit him in such a warm, vulnerable spot. The shotgun in his hands went off and sprayed buckshot in the trees above us.

I twisted to yell at Jim Luke to run, but he wasn't there. "You dirty, damn coward, Jim Luke," I screeched, and crawled as fast as I could until I got to the darkness under the trees. Then I ran like hell, yelling, "You're a chicken, dirty coward, Jim Luke!"

I had run and hollered myself out by the time I got back to our own barn lot. There, big as life, sat Jim Luke on the rail fence of the barnyard. I wasn't even going to stop or speak to him, but he reached out and grabbed me as I passed and spun me around.

"Get you hands off'n me, you chicken coward. A runnin' off and a leavin' me!" I yelled before he had time to slap his hand over my mouth.

"Shut up, Sammy John. Listen. We gotta go spy on some more folks," he said.

"You shut your mouth, Jim Luke. I ain't going no-where else so's you can run off and leave me again. 'Sides, it was probably old Zack that killed that man any-how, a thinkin' he was gonna steal his dad-blamed chickens." I gasped, running out of breath.

"No, it wasn't," Jim Luke said, " 'cause couldn't you see old Zack is too old and weak to of carried him and poked him down the tree? So we gotta go look some-wheres else."

"Well, you go on if you want to, but my toes is nigh froze off and I ain't a goin' nowhere again tonight, 'cep-tin' to bed!" I told him, and headed toward our win-dow.

Jim Luke trotted to keep up with me, hissing, "How would you like for me to beat the living hell out'n you?"

"Well, I reckon you can, since you're bigger'n me, but when you get finished I'm still goin' to bed."

"Oh, I didn't mean that, Sammy. Aw come on. We could spy on somebody afore daylight and maybe get the killer and money sooner. Come on," he said.

"No! I'm a goin' to bed!" I hissed back, and stepped back through the window and under the covers without taking off my britches. In a few minutes Jim Luke fol-lowed me. We didn't talk, since I was still sore at Jim Luke for running, but when I thought about it some I knew deep down that I would have run off and left him if I had thought of it first. So I turned and whispered, "We'll go tomorrow night, Jim Luke." He didn't say anything, but punched me on the shoulder with his fist, so I snuggled further down under the covers. We were friends again and we were going to be rich, me and Jim Luke.

26

CHAPTER 4

Spying was knocked right out of our heads the next morning when Grandpa told us at breakfast that Uncle Shall was coming with his truck to take us to the river for the last time before winter. In a whirl of excitement we rushed through the chores and started digging grub and red worms for fishing. If there was anything me and Jim Luke liked better than the river and fishing, it was getting to ride on the back of Uncle Shall's truck. We didn't have a car of any kind, and the only time we ever got to ride in one was when one of the kinfolk took us some place.

Man, oh man, didn't we feel proud passing the farms of folks we knew and waving at them. The truck went so much faster than our sled with old Ned pulling it, and it nearly took our breath away. Jim Luke would point out neighbor girls and sneer, boy, how he would like to spark that one. And he'd ask me, with a poke in the ribs, if I would too. I always said I'd be cat haired if I wouldn't, but Jim Luke never got around to telling me what sparking was about, and I never asked, though I had a sneaking hunch that Jim Luke was powerfully earthy in his feelings.

We were ready and waiting with our cans full of worms and our poles in our hands when Uncle Shall drove up in his old red truck. Uncle Shall was married to Jim Luke's sister, Aunt Imie. Aunt Imie was fat with really tiny legs, lie a bird, and she dipped snuff and gossiped a lot.

Uncle Shall was short and square. Even his head looked square. Me and Jim Luke knew he spent a mighty lot of time with the hill women and tried to stay around the one Grandma called "the old bad girl" down the hill from where we lived. We never told though, because Uncle Shall would take us just about any place if he was going there anyhow.

"Hop in, boys," he called when he drove up, and we threw our poles on the flat bed and bounced up after them. Grandpa got in the cab with him, and after waving to Grandma we tore off down the hill. We hung onto the cab and each other as Uncle Shall took the curves at what to us was breathing-taking speed. The roads were narrow and twisting and were nearly all downhill. In about ten miles the road flattened out some, and going around the last tree-shaded curve there she was, good old Buffalo River, wide and sluggish in its banks, flat with sand sparkling white against the blue water in the sun.

Uncle Shall stopped the truck under the trees just before we reached the sand. It was still too cold and early in the morning for our last swim of the summer, so me and Jim Luke baited our hooks and threw them out in the river while Granpa and Uncle Shall hunted wood, built a fire and put coffee on in an old black coffeepot. Then they, too, sat down beside us, tossing their lines in. Lord, I could almost taste brown, fried fish with corn bread and green onions Grandma always sent, and the cups of steaming coffee that me and Jim Luke only got to drink when we were with the men, fishing.

Jim Luke caught a good-sized trout. He baited his hook and flung it back in. Nobody ever talked much until after the first fish was caught, then everybody relaxed and opened up.

Grandpa and Uncle Shall talked about crops, mending fences and what they were going to plant next year.

28

They got kind of dirty about breeding the cows and horses. It was good listening.

Everybody was happy, and suddenly I had an overwhelming urge to confide in them about the dead man in the tree. Then a terrifying thought hit me, what if Grandpa or Uncle Shall had killed him? I couldn't think of any good reason for Grandpa doing it, but Uncle Shall might. Maybe the dead man was the husband of the old bad girl down the hill from us. Maybe he had caught Uncle Shall, and Uncle Shall had killed him and poked him in the tree.

I was about to kill myself making faces at Jim Luke. I was trying to convey to him that I had to see him alone, when Uncle Shall brought in the biggest catfish I had ever seen. All of us were helping to pull him in. After we admired it and walked around and fingered it, Grandpa and Uncle Shall took it and Jim Luke's trout to clean and start cooking.

When me and Jim Luke were alone I told him what I had thought about Uncle Shall killing our man in the tree. After I finished, out of breath, I watched Jim Luke. He studied on it a long time then he said, "Well, they's jist one thing to do. We gotta go see the old bad girl."

"But Jim Luke," I protested, "you know Grandma'd whop the daylights out'n us iffen she found out we talked to her."

"I don't care, Sammy John, and 'sides, we gotta ask her iffen she was ever wed. And if we slip through the orchard nobody can see us," he said.

"Listen, Jim Luke. What if Uncle Shall did kill that man? We couldn't turn him in. Could we, Jim Luke?" I reached out to shake him, then got scared because that dad-blamed Jim Luke would do almost anything for money.

He turned and grinned at me. "Nah," he said, "I wouldn't do that, but maybe we would get a reward for just finding the dead man." Then he said, "Boy, oh boy, smell them fish a fryin'. Let's go eat." I stuck my pole in the sand and followed him.

After we ate we took off our britches and laid in the sun, naked as the day we were born, drowsing and trying to soak up enough of the warm sunlight for the winter ahead. Grandpa and Uncle Shall went back to fishing for a mess to take home.

"You know, Sammy John," Jim Luke said, sleepily, staring at his private parts, or what we called ding dongs, "I got a purty big'un."

I sniggered, "It might be a big'un but it shore ain't purty, Jim Luke." He laughed too.

"Yeah," he said, "but man, iffen it was fifteen feet long I could stand outside under the trees and let it creep around the corner of a house into some old gal's winder afore she knowed what was a happenin'." I sniggered again.

"Yeah, man," I said, "and she could grab a hoe and chop its head off, mistakin' it fer a snake afore you could grab it back. 'Sides, what you want to poke somethin' like that in a winder fer?"

"Ye seen our animals a matin', ain't ye, Sammy?" he asked.

"Yep, and you don't have to sound so high and mighty. I know they's a doin' it and I know why—to get little'uns. And man, I don't want no little'uns fer I can't take care of myself real good yet. So there," I said.

"Oh shut up, Sammy, you jist wait till you get as old as me. You don't know the half of nothin', and I bet you still believe in Santa Claus," he said.

"I don't neither," I holled at him, and jumped up running for the bluff at the river's edge. Jim Luke's heels pounded hard behind me. He couldn't even stand for me to get ahead of him.

We dove off of the bluff into the water. After we stopped shaking and turning blue, the water felt warm, and we yelled and ducked each other and swam until Grandpa called us and made us put our britches on over our protests to let us stay in for just five minutes more.

Jim Luke whispered to hurry, that maybe we would get home in time to go see the old bad girl. But when we did get home, Grandpa made us clean the fish he and Uncle Shall had caught. Then Uncle Shall went to get Aunt Imie to come and eat supper with her folks. It was near sunset when we got to slip through the orchard. Aunt Imie was still at the house, and she would keep Grandpa and Grandma talking so they wouldn't miss us. Uncle Shall had gone to the store, about seven miles away, for coal oil, and would pick up Aunt Imie on his way back.

The old bad woman's house was small, but painted white with green window trim. Her yard was big and clean, with hollyhocks blooming red, white and pink all around a white picket fence. Jim Luke's eyes were tiny slits, and we marched straight up to the door. We had never seen the old bad woman up close, and thought anybody as bad as the women whispered that she was would likely look like a witch.

I didn't know it then, but all hill women hate and mistrust city women. They think if a woman wears make-up or smokes, she is a hell-bound, no-good tool of the devil. I think they are afraid of their well-dressed good looks and are afraid their menfolks will stray (and they do every chance they get).

Most hill women dress in long, cotton dresses, and they, themselves, are faded and old before their time from too much childbearing and hard field work. So they talk about women from the city in hopes of making their menfolks think they are the devil's imps to scare them into leaving the city women alone. Really, they more or less drive their men to them because a soft, red, lipsticked mouth looks ever so much nicer than lips dripping snuff juice at the corners and most hill women dip snuff.

The girl who opened the door at Jim Luke's knock was young, not over twenty at the most, and she was very pretty with the coal-oil lamplight shining on her hair. It nearly stopped our hearts beating. She just stood

31

there smiling at us with her pretty white teeth showing through lips as red as strawberries. Her skin was the color of the cream that raised in Grandma's jars for butter, her eyes were the color of dark brown pansies, and she smelled like the lilac bushes growing in Wiley Brewer's yard. Her hair looked like thick, foggy mist, with the lamplight shooting red and copper streaks through it. She was slim, not much taller than Jim Luke, and wore blue jeans with a red checked shirt. She was barefoot. Suddenly, as she stood there smiling at us, I felt the most awful, hurting, lonesome pain for my mother that I had tried to push into the farthest part of my mind since she went away. Before I could help it I felt tears come to my eyes.

I don't know what Jim Luke felt, but he was breathing hard like he had been running, and he gasped even harder when she spoke in a voice as soft and sweet as a breeze blowing through the pine treetops.

"Hello, boys," she said, "is there something I can do for you?"

"Yes'm," we muttered. We looked at each other, not knowing exactly what to say. Jim Luke tried to dig his big toe into the porch and kind of cleared his throat a time or two.

Finally I piped up with, "Well, ma'm, this is a sociable call, ya might say we's jist bein' neighborly."

She looked at us for a minute and I could see the corners of her mouth twitch slightly as if she were trying to hide a grin.

"Well, in that case, won't you come in? This is the first 'sociable' call I've had in a long time."

"Yes'm," we muttered, edging through the door.

"Would you like to sit down?" she asked.

"No'm, I mean yes'm," I gulped as Jim Luke's sharp elbow took me in the ribs. We sat on the couch and looked around big eyed. She disappeared through a door into what looked like a kitchen. I could see the corner of a table from where I sat. When she went out of the room she seemed to take half of the light with her.

Her house was as pretty as she was. There was a fire burning in a stone fireplace, rag rugs were scattered over shining wood floors, white curtains hung at the windows, and the whole room was a mixture of cleanness and bright colors.

In a minute she was back with a plate of sugar cookies and three big mugs of cold milk. She put them on the table in front of us and drew up a rocking chair for herself. She smiled at us, picked up a cooky and bit into it with her pretty white teeth, then motioned for us to do the same.

I felt powerfully unclean, and for the first time I could actually smell Jim Luke. We were so dirty we stunk, and I wished we had worn our Sunday pants and striped shirts that Grandma had made out of flour sacks.

After we had eaten and drunk the milk, she leaned back, lit a cigarette and smiled. "Okay, boys," she said, "to what do I owe the honor of your visit?" The sight of her smoking had made us lose our voices again. "And by the way," she continued, "my name is Raven Megan, what's yours?"

"Jim Luke, ma'm, and this here's Sammy John," Jim Luke croaked, nearly poking my eye out as he pointed at me. "Well, ma'm . . ." he started, but she cut him off.

"Please call me Raven. The ma'm makes me feel old." She smiled at Jim Luke.

He swallowed so hard I thought he was going to choke on his Adam's apple, but he got it out, "All right, Raven Megan." I knew he was calling her both names so he could get on the good side of her, and I decided to do the same the first chance I got. "We come to see if you be wed," he said.

She looked startled for a moment, then laughed. "No, I not be wed. Why? Did you wish to propose?" That shut Jim Luke up like a clam with a red face.

Then I jumped in with, "No ma'm, I mean Raven Megan, we can't be wed yet 'cause Grandma won't let

33

us, but iffen we could we'd be mighty pleased for it to be you." I took a deep breath.

She smiled a little mistily and said softly, "Thank you, Sammy John."

Jim Luke stuck himself in again with, "Raven Megan, we was jist curious if you be wed to a red-headed man."

"No, gentlemen, why do you ask? I have never been wed or even had a red-headed boy friend. Now you're making me curious."

"I reckon we can't talk with you no more," Jim Luke said fast and sharp. It startled everybody.

Then Raven Megan's lips sort of quivered and her eyes filmed over with tears. "Why?" she asked in a quivering voice. "Did your grandmother tell you not to talk to me?"

"No ma'm," I spoke too fast.

"She's not my grandmother," Jim Luke hurriedly put in, "but my ma."

"Well, I know what the women around her say about me," Raven Megan said, trying to smile, but her lips were still quivering.

"We don't care, we don't care at all. We think you are the prettiest thing ever," Jim Luke and I spoke nearly at the same time.

We looked at each other, our faces red. How were we going to explain to her that if she would get fat and dip snuff, the hill women would accept her? How could we explain to ourselves the sudden trusting we had in our hearts for her? It was not just her prettiness, or cleanliness, it was her way of accepting us for ourselves and inviting us into her home, even after being shunned by everyone she encountered.

As if she read our minds, she said, "It's so nice for you to care, and I'm honored that you think I'm pretty. However, I wouldn't want to be the reason for you getting into trouble with your family. There must be a reason you wanted to know if I were married. Please tell me what it is. There appears to be more to this than

34

meets the eye, to make you go where you have been forbidden to go."

I felt like I would burst, wanting to tell her everything, needing to tell someone I could trust, because it was weighing me down. I looked at Jim Luke and could tell he was feeling the same way. We had found a murdered man, we didn't know who he was or who he knew. We didn't even know why he was killed.

Yet, Raven Megan was new here; we knew everyone else. Was she just pumping us for information, or was she just trying to be friendly? We didn't know. Should we just get up and leave or should we stay and tell her a lie, anything to satisfy her until we knew she didn't have anything to do with it?

Raven Megan sat quietly, studying us with those big brown eyes. Somehow I knew everyone else was wrong and we were right. I would trust her with my very life.

Without knowing when or how, we were both on our knees by her chair looking up at her and babbling out how we had found a dead man in the tree, why we wanted the reward money and why we had come to see her. We talked to late hours, until the lamp burned out.

At first she stared at us as if we had lost our minds. Then she laughed and said, "Forgive me, it's not funny for a man to lose his life, but it just occurred to me how funny it would be for me to spy on my neighbors and help you find the killer. It seems that everyone knows everything about me, but I know nothing about any of them. I know this isn't right, I should report this, but somehow I feel like keeping this secret and helping. Maybe when we do find the killer things will change. I can just imagine what would happen to me now if I opened my mouth anyway." She crossed her heart and hoped to die before she would tell our secret.

The grin faded from her lips though as she said, "It is so sad that women can be so malicious and mean when they don't understand someone who dresses or acts different than they do. The men are friendly," she laughed bitterly, "but I suspect not in the way they would be to a

35

respectable woman. All I wanted to do was find someplace where it was quiet so I could relax and write a book. I just might enjoy this little episode after all."

"Raven Megan," Jim Luke said, "Sammy John here and me, we'll allus be your friends. We'll come and get you the next time we go to spy on someone."

"Okay, Jim Luke," she said, "I'll be waiting."

Feeling proud, we muttered, "Good night, Raven Megan," and never felt our feet hit the ground all the way home. We were both a little in love for the first time in our lives, at least I was, but from the way Jim Luke twisted and turned I figured he was more in heat, because if that Jim Luke was anything, he was earthy.

I felt a big sigh of relief clear to my toes. I was glad that Uncle Shall took Raven Megan chopped stovewood, because it was hill hospitality for the men to do this for a woman alone, but I was glad that was all he did. I was also relieved to know that me and Jim Luke had a grownup on our side.

CHAPTER 5

The next day, being Sunday, we couldn't do much about our dead man because Sundays were the days Jim Luke's married brothers and sisters came to spend the day. The one good thing about it was that they brought all kinds of good things to eat, even store-bought bread and bologna, my very favorite food. It was sure a good change from beans, potatoes and old Bessy.

We thought some about spying on them, for sisters or not, Jim Luke wanted that money bad to get a race horse and guns. Having Raven Megan on our side still gave us a warm glow, and all day we kept poking each other in the ribs and grinning whenever we thought of her.

Grandma and my aunts started right away to talk about her, saying things like "No woman is any good that'll wear them fancy clothes and paint her face. Mark my words, she's out after every man she can get." Or when they would do anything, they would say, "Catch Miss Fancy Britches workin' her lily white hands like this. Like as not we'd be pizened from all that reddenin' on her fingernails."

It made us mad, but we didn't dare say anything.

We had known Jim Luke's brothers and sisters, my aunts and uncles, all our lives, but finding the dead man in the tree made us take a new look at them. It was sort of like we had never seen them before. We hung around the women, eating our bologna sandwiches, listening and trying to look like we weren't.

There was a whole houseful of them, and babies crawled all over the place. Some were walking, and some were so little they had to be held or laid on the beds. No wonder the menfolks gathered in the barn where they could hear themselves talk, I thought, as I looked the women over. I couldn't say I liked any of them much, and I knew Jim Luke wasn't exactly overcome with brotherly love either. Of course, maybe it was because he had been born after they all had gone. He often said that all he had left was a dried-up tit. But I knew one thing for sure, as mean as he was, he loved Grandpa and Grandma.

I walked over close to where Lena and Rena were talking. Lena was letting a baby suck. Rena was leaning close to her saying, "I tell you, Lena, it's a durn good thing I'm not hot natured or it would kill poor old Homer." I didn't know what she meant, but I knew Uncle Homer was old. There had been a big fight, and Jim Luke said Grandma didn't want Rena to marry him since he was twenty-five years older than her. Grandpa didn't care because Uncle Homer always brought him a big mess of catfish when he came to call on Rena.

Looking at her sticking-out gooseberry eyes and stringy, straw-colored hair, I figured she was lucky to get anybody at all. I sure hoped she never got hot natured or whatever it was. Uncle Homer was the best fisherman on Buffalo River, and I didn't want to see him go.

Lena was a copy of Rena, except for being a lot taller. "I tell you, I can't stand for Less to tech me neither," Lena said. "In fact, I'd druther a snake bit me. But I'll tell you what ye can do. . . ." And then she noticed me. "Sammy John, git outside where you belong! Now git!" She nearly made me choke on a bite of bologna, but I went to find Jim Luke in the other room. I sat by him behind Aunt Imie, Opal and Flo. Opal and Flo were the wives of Jim Luke's brothers, Lester and Ed.

I leaned over and hissed in Jim Luke's ear, "Hey, you know what? Aunt Lena thinks Uncle Less is worse than a snake."

"Shut up," Jim Luke said, "you ain't heard nothin' yet. Be quiet so's they don't notice us."

I shut up and settled back to listen. They first sounded like a bunch of hens clucking, then words started coming through. But I didn't hear much until Jim Luke started poking me because I was watching Aunt Opal poking her tit in a young'ns mouth, and she had the longest tits I had ever seen. I'll bet they were two feet long. The kid sucking it was so big he stood on the floor at her knees and sucked like crazy, and I knew that dad-blamed kid could talk and had a full set of teeth.

Then the mistiness cleared up when Jim Luke poked me. Aunt Imie was saying, "I swan Opal, when ya gonna wean that young'n?" The young'n they were talking about rolled his eyes from one to the other but never let go of the tit.

I could almost see him relax when Aunt Opal answered, "Well, I don't know. 'Course ya know as long as ya let one suck you can't get pregnant again."

I even knew what that meant, for Jim Luke told me every time a cow or horse was that way it meant that before long there would be a little one around. I figured Aunt Opal had plenty of sense because she already had eight young'ns.

"Well, I don't know about that," Aunt Flo started, " 'cause when I had Dale Even . . . Lord a mercy, Jim Luke, Sammy John, how long you been here? Git out of here! Ma, Ma make them boys git outside!" But we didn't wait for Grandma to holler, we went through the kitchen, grabbed another hunk of bologna and bread, then headed for the barn and the men.

When we came up they were looking at a stud horse Grandpa had borrowed to service our old mare. I looked Uncle Less over trying to see where he resembled a snake. He did have sort of beady eyes and a long nose, but I couldn't see that he looked like a snake. The men said something about the stud and laughed, then started talking crops, so me and Jim Luke finished our sandwiches and went to sit on the porch and rub old Salt and Pepper and to think of Raven Megan and sneaking out tonight to spy on our neighbors. Jim Luke said he reckoned we ought to take a nap so we'd be wide awake when it got dark. Then we laid back on the porch with the dogs.

I didn't figure I would ever get to sleep, but the afternoon sun crept up my legs, warming them, and made me drowsy. Jim Luke started snoring, lulling me still further and further. I didn't know anything else until the kinfolks came pouring out of the house, hollering, "Bye" and dragging the little ones by the hand.

Uncle Shall poked Jim Luke in the ribs with the toe of his shoe, nearly making Jim Luke jump clean off the porch. Of course, he didn't know we had a right to be spooky.

The sun was going down and we hurried through the chores as fast as we could, hoping Grandpa and Grandma would be all tired out from company and go to bed early, so we could sneak out. Every time we caught them looking at us we yawned big, hoping to make them sleepy. It didn't work, so me and Jim Luke ate the rest of the bologna.

Catching a wink from Jim Luke, I got Grandpa and Grandma to talking about my pa when he was young so Jim Luke could sneak Grandpa's flashlight, some matches, some food and a sack. In case we had to be out late we didn't want Raven Megan to get hungry or scared. Besides, Grandpa and Grandma always liked to tell me about my pa, and usually I liked hearing about him. Tonight, I only listened with one ear, the other was on Jim Luke.

Grandpa had just come to the part in the story about my pa running away from home to live in the woods and coon hunt when Jim Luke came in and said we had to get some sleep if we were going to get up early and clean out Ed Watson's pond. I followed him to bed as if

40

I knew what he was talking about. I knew it was just an excuse, and besides I had heard the story about my pa running off so many times I knew it by heart.

I wished I could be that brave. When my pa was thirteen, he got tired of farm work and ran away to the woods just taking his dog, gun and some salt, and lived for two weeks on squirrels and whatever else he could kill, and berries he picked. But Grandpa said he reckoned Pa was glad to get home, once Grandpa tracked him down, because he settled down and made the best farm worker of all Grandpa's children, and never complained about working again.

Me and Jim Luke laid on the bed with our clothes on, waiting for the old folks to bed down, not even daring to whisper for fear we would keep them awake. Excitement gnawed in me again at the thought of having Raven Megan with us, and I kept wondering who we were going to spy on tonight. A thought crept into my mind that if we didn't hurry and find the killer, everybody that passed within a hundred yards of that tree would know something dead was in it. It made me nearly sick thinking of it, so I tried hard to get my thoughts back on Raven Megan.

Thoughts of my ma drowned them out, and I wondered how she was and what kind of work she was doing, and when she would be able to send for me. Sometimes I had to think with all my might to remember what she looked like. I knew she had dark eyes with hair like me, but tonight I couldn't remember whether she was little or big, but remembered her smelling good like Raven Megan. I sure would like to have seen my ma, but hated the thought of leaving Jim Luke too. I felt ashamed when my eyes got hot, so I rubbed them hard and yawned like I was getting sleepy in case Jim Luke was looking. Then I relaxed because it was so dark he couldn't see me anyhow.

There was no light under our door any more, and that meant Grandpa and Grandma had gone to bed. We hardly moved until we heard Grandpa start to snore, then Jim Luke pulled out the sack of stuff he had stashed under the bed, and we again slipped through the window. We were halfway through the orchard before we dared to talk.

"Jim Luke, who are we gonna spy on tonight?" I asked low.

"The new doc," he hissed back, not turning his head.

"The new doc?! Jim Luke, you know good and well iffen the doc killed the man he would cut him up or say he died natural or somethin'," I said. "I sure can't see a doctor pokin' a body down an old tree."

"Sammy John, you're stupid. That's just it, nobody but me would suspect a doctor of killin' a body like that. 'Sides, if Raven Megan gets scared or faints or somethin' we'll be near a doctor. And now, don't talk so much, you want everybody in the country to hear us 'round about?"

I didn't bother to answer him, but reckoned to myself we would sure have some explaining to do if Raven Megan did faint. Of course, we could always tell the doctor we were just passing by or something if she did. But then, she didn't look like the fainting type to me. And the doc didn't look easily fooled either.

He was kind of new hereabouts; hadn't even been here as long as me. He came from a city someplace, and took over all of Doctor Passmore's practice when the old doc died of old age, and Grandpa said from a pickled liver from drinking his own alcohol.

The young doc was only thirty years old or so. He had come to take care of me and Jim Luke when we had whooping cough, and we had been friends since. All of my aunts and Jim Luke's sisters called him the "pretty doc." He was tall, taller than the other men around, and his blue eyes got all crinkly when he laughed. His name was Doctor Jason McCoy. I had seen it on his door. He lived about six miles north of us in the same house where the old doc had lived. It looked the same except for a long building he had built, and he called his laboratory. I also liked to fool around there because he

42

studied ticks and wild animals in cages like rabbits, squirrels and even mice. When he wasn't busy helping the womenfolks get babies or sometimes helping the farmers with cows and sheep or anything hurting, he was in that laboratory. I sure hoped he wasn't the killer, because I liked him just fine, and helped him catch rabbits and things when I had time.

I watched Jim Luke pick his way carefully through the orchard and guessed he liked money better than almost anybody or anything. Then I felt bad for I knew I wanted money just as bad.

It wasn't as light as the night before, but it was getting so, for the full moon was rising higher and I could feel the cold mist of frost start biting my toes. Me and Jim Luke just got one pair of shoes a year, and then just before school started. I'd be doggoned glad when the time came. My feet had been getting mighty cold lately. The frost always made the persimmons sweet and juicy, and I could hear them falling with fat plops, and would have liked to stop and eat some but hurried to catch up with Jim Luke. I bet the possums were out in full force on a night like this.

There was a lamp burning in Raven Megan's house, and she had the door open before Jim Luke had barely tapped. She had on pretty, short, black boots, tight blue jeans, a red jacket, and was prettier and sweeter smelling than I remembered.

"I got you some bread and stuff in here," Jim Luke muttered, poking the sack out to her.

She smiled and said, "Thank you, Jim Luke, you are a most thoughtful gentleman." Jim Luke turned red and swelled up proud and told her he reckoned we'd better hit the trail if we were going to catch a killer. I felt like kicking him. He sounded like he was going to catch the killer all by himself and just for her. I sort of wished I had thought about the food myself, but I could tell from the whiff when he opened the sack that he had brought some of old Bessy between biscuits. I wondered if Raven Megan would eat the meat if she knew it had been named.

"Let's go, men," Raven Megan whispered to us. "Now we can't do much talking because sound carries on a clear night like this."

"I'll lead," said Jim Luke, "you come next and Sammy John can bring up the rear, so iffen somethin' happens we can protect you."

With that he led off with his shoulders back, the sack slung over one of them. I was sore and thought, "Protect hell. Iffen that Jim Luke runs the way he did last night when old Zack's gun went off, it'll be me doin' the protecting." Thinking that made me feel better, but I nearly had to run to keep up.

Jim Luke knew just where we were going, and Raven Megan was sure-footed and fast. She was the first female I ever knew that could keep her mouth shut. She didn't say a word until we got to the doctor's place, then she only gasped a little with surprise when the moon came out showing where we were. The moonlight showed almost as bright as day around Doc's white-painted fence and house, but no light shined through the window. Doc's was the only place in the hills that had a phone, and its wires looked strange and out of place.

Jim Luke put his finger to his lips, dropped to his knees and crawled fast under the trees from where we stood, until he was in the shadow near the fence. Without a word, Raven Megan dropped and crawled after him. So there was nothing left for me to do but follow.

We crawled around the fence until we could see his laboratory in the back. Sure enough, light showed through its windows and we could see Doc pass back and forth in a white coat. Raven Megan was staring at him so hard that Jim Luke had to poke her twice before she would follow him up next to the wall. I knew he wanted to look through the window. So did I, but first I crawled up against Raven's head and whispered into her ear, "You know the doc?"

"Just slightly," she whispered back. "I met him once

when he came to set my ankle when I sprained it falling in a hole."

I wanted to ask her what kind of a hole, but about that time Jim Luke nearly knocked the breath out of me and hissed, "Shhh, shhh," so I crawled back behind her and kept quiet.

We barely breathed when we got under the window, and had to hug the wall so the lamplight wouldn't fall on us. The window was about neck high to Jim Luke, but I had to stretch with all my might just to get my eyes even with the window sill. Raven Megan crouched a little and so did Jim Luke. At the same time we raised our eyes and peered, then ducked again and almost ran, for two beady pink eyes were staring back straight at us. It took a few fast breaths to reveal the thing staring at us was a rabbit, held in Doc's hands as he bent his head over it poking a needle into its hind end. The rabbit squealed and twisted a little, but when Doc pulled out the needle he petted and rubbed the rabbit gently before putting him back in the cage. He walked over to a sink and started soaping and washing his hands.

The black telephone hanging on the wall next to the door rang. He hurriedly dried his hands and answered it. We couldn't hear what he was saying, but as soon as he hung up he reached for a black bag, grabbed a coat from a nail and took off the white coat before putting it on. My hands started slipping from the window sill and Raven Megan caught at me before I hit the ground. The last glance I had of Doc, he was standing at the window. We all hit the ground on our knees and shot around the corner of the house and behind the picket fence just as he came out of the door carrying his black bag. Without a glance behind him that we could see, he walked down the road in the moonlight.

Breathing easy because he hadn't seen us after all, we eased out after him, keeping to the edge of the trees that grew thick near the road, so if he happened to look back we could slip into the shadows. We were breathing fast, and even Raven Megan seemed to be excited. I felt

45

we must have been on a hot trail, and could tell Jim Luke felt the same because where in the world would a body be going this late at night. Even Doc. If anybody around was sick we would have heard it that day when the kinfolks all came, because nothing went on that some of them didn't know.

Doc started whistling a happy, cheerful tune, and the first thing I knew we were keeping in step with it. I tried to quit and walk natural, but it didn't work so I just quit fighting it and started enjoying it. The world seemed unreal, the doc striding and whistling, with moonlight making gold streaks on top of his head, and us high stepping it under the darkened shade of the trees made it more like a visit into dreamland.

I don't really know how long we walked, but it was Jim Luke peering ahead who hissed, "Drop! It's Rudy Spraddle's place." Me and Raven Megan hit the dirt just as Doc flung off the road and went toward a ramshackled house that was unpainted and looked like one with the dark wood, except for the gleam of lamplight coming faintly through the rear window. Dogs set up barking at Doc, and Jim Luke whispered, "Run nigh the house so they'll think the dog is only barkin' at Doc." We ran close to the ground, and Raven Megan was giggling and enjoying herself fit to kill.

We felt our way to the back of the house where the lamplight showed through the window stronger, and lay flat against the ground gasping to get our breath back. We could hear voices coming out of the window. Three panes were broken out. We heard one of the Spraddle gals moan in the bedroom, "Doc, her time done come." Doc's voice was kind and sort of soft, saying not to worry, he would see about it.

For some reason I started breaking up in giggles and Jim Luke flew over and sat on me, holding his hand over my mouth till I nearly died from lack of breath. No doubt I would have, but Raven Megan pulled him off of me. I took a deep breath, but still had an urge to giggle because just the other day Grandma had said to Grandpa that old Rudy Spraddle kept Sally Lou with one a comin', one a crawlin' and one a carryin'. The Spraddles had more young ones than anybody around abouts; fourteen at last count.

Rudy was a thin, pale, skinny little man with bug eyes, and Sally Lou was five times bigger than him, cheerful, comfortable and constantly pregnant. Rudy made moonshine and his young'ns planted a few crops, just enough to get them by with what meat Rudy killed, in season or out.

And now we had followed Doc all this way just to bring another Spraddle into this world.

I could tell Raven Megan thought it was funny too. But Jim Luke was sorely disappointed because his hopes had been high on catching the killer. We edged around a corner and raised up to peer into a back room. Sally Lou was laying spread-legged on the bed and Doc was holding her hand, talking and laughing. Once in a while Sally Lou drew her legs up and sort of moaned sad and hurtful. I was ready to leave, and I think Raven Megan was too. We tugged at Jim Luke, but he wouldn't budge. So all we knew to do was stay and watch also.

Our eyes were glued to the twisting woman on the bed. She had the biggest belly I had ever seen. We heard Doc yell through the bedroom door, "Sarah Jane, where's your pa?"

"He'll be back afore long, Doc," a stringy-haired, fourteen-year-old stuck her head around the door and yelled, "he went to call you over to Jackson's store, so reckon it'll take him a while." I could see Doc's frowning when the woman on the bed drew up her legs again.

She was covered with papers of some sort. The bedstead was like ours, made out of iron. The wall was papered with faded flowers and it was hanging in places in the corners where water circles showed that it leaked. On another bed two little girls, about one and three, slept like nothing in the world was happening.

It was the stiff, scared way Jim Luke and Raven Megan were standing that drew my eyes from the bed,

47

straight up to Doc's eyes where he was standing just at the side of the window, staring, grinning and looking at us. I froze too. Lord, if he was the killer he had us now. With one long stride he had the window open, leaned out and said coldly, "Raven Megan, and gentlemen," nodding coldly at me and Jim Luke, "if you are quite finished following me and spying and lurking around the house, I could use your help in here."

For a little while I thought none of us were going to talk again. Finally Jim Luke swallowed a few times and started to, but Raven Megan put her hand on his shoulder and spoke up herself, and I sure admired her dignity. "Of course," she said back to the doc just as cool as he had spoken, "just tell me what needs to be done." Then she swung her legs over the window sill and slid gracefully into the room.

Doc leaned out, glaring at me and Jim Luke. "You two find the woodpile and chop some wood, then draw some water from the well and heat it." Before we could answer one way or the other, he slammed the window in our faces, and to add insult to our already shameful predicament, he threw some kind of cloth over it so we couldn't see in any more.

Jim Luke cussed steadily as we located the chopping block and started chopping wood. He was so mad I reckon he cut more wood that night than Rudy had cut all winter and summer put together. When we carried it to the back door of the house, Raven Megan met us, took the wood, and wouldn't even let us in. We sat dejected on the chopping block, feeling that even Raven Megan had gone against us. Jim Luke quit cussing when Sarah Jane came out and sat beside him on the block of wood. I was tired and kept dropping off in a light doze only to be brought out of it by Jim Luke sort of sniggering and Sarah Jane squealing, "Stop that, Jim Luke, now you stop it." It was too dark for me to see what Jim Luke was doing, but I could tell by the sound of Sarah Jane's voice that she didn't really want him to stop.

I must have really dropped off, because I came fully

awake with Raven Megan calling out of the door for us to come and see something. Jim Luke and Sarah Jane sort of slunk in behind me. In the light Jim Luke's face was red, and Sarah Jane kept sneaking looks at him and giggling. Raven Megan led the way to the bedroom where Doc held a bundle and Sally Lou looked proud and peaceful. Doc's face was gentle as he opened the blanket and showed us a red, wrinkled baby.

"Pa'll surely be glad of another boy," said Sally Lou.

"Then where's he at?" Raven Megan sort of snapped.

"Oh, Pa allus hides out until after birthin'," laughed Sally Lou cheerfully.

Hill people always call their spouses Ma and Pa.

I just kept watching Doc's face. His eyes were kind of shining, and he looked like a man who had just eaten all the fried chicken he wanted. I mean all happy like. He saw me looking at him and grinned.

"You just couldn't have murdered nobody," I blurted out. Shock went over his face. I didn't know Raven Megan and Jim Luke had heard me until Doc started to say something and she took hold of his elbow and stepped on my toe to boot. But Sally Lou and Sarah Jane weren't paying any attention, they were looking over the baby Doc had laid on the bed beside Sally Lou. Almost everybody had something good to say about the baby but me and Jim Luke. I figured he was going to kill me as soon as we were alone for he was worried about me blabbing to the doc.

Nobody said anything until we got to the doc's house. He made coffee and we all sat around the kitchen table. He gave me and Jim Luke a thick coffee cup filled with milk, lots of sugar and very little coffee.

"Now," he said, taking his own chair, "I want the truth. I saw you following me, and wanted to see how far you would go. Now I'd like to know why you find it so interesting to follow me in the first place. I know things get pretty dull around here, but I've never before had anyone to sneak out at night just to see what I'm up to. How about it, boys?"

"Wal, Doc, ya see, Sammy here has a powerful urge to ask ye somethin'," Jim Luke muttered, "and seein' as how ya caught us followin' ya I guess maybe he oughta get on with it. Sammy?"

"Uh, well Doc, ya see . . ." I started.

"Well?" he asked.

Jim Luke nudged me and I said, "Oh Doc, you wouldn't kill nobody, would you? Would you, Doc?"

He looked at me in a funny way and said, "Well, I don't know, Sammy, I never had any reason to kill anyone, and I don't think I could. However, there are circumstances where people have killed when they had to, like in a war. To just come right out and kill someone —no, I don't think I could."

And as stern as he said it, I knew he meant just what he said. So, Jim Luke told him about us finding the body in the tree and Raven Megan told how we had come to her and why she was with us. Things were sort of hazy because I was never so tired in my life. Jim Luke's big ears were beginning to droop, and he couldn't talk very straight either.

Both of us perked up when Doc started talking about calling the sheriff. Jim Luke yelled that he had no right. The body was ours. Then, I'm ashamed to say, I started crying and blubbering about how I had to have the reward money so me and my ma could be together again.

Then Raven Megan was arguing on our side saying, "Please, Doc, these boys are only trying to find out who killed the man. They don't even know who he is, and at first they thought he might have something to do with me."

"Well, that's all the more reason why we should call the sheriff," he said, "let him handle it. He has the means of finding out who he is and what he's doing here." He started for the phone.

Jim Luke got up and grabbed hold of Doc's arm. He said, "Please, Doc, just give us a little bit longer. This means a lot to us, findin' that killer. If we let everybody know, they's no tellin' what-n-all would happen then.

Maybe someone else would get killed. Maybe even me and Sammy here. Oh Doc, ya don't understand. People around here hold grudges and—ya gotta help us, Doc, you just gotta."

Then suddenly Doc said all right, but to let him bring the body and put it somewhere cold or there wouldn't be anything left but bones by the time we found the killer, and he would do an autopsy or something to find out how he was killed. Finally we all said all right.

A little dejectedly Jim Luke brought out the now crumpled sack with the biscuits and old Bessy. Nobody ate much. When I nearly fell off my chair Doc said, "I'll get the car and take you all home."

"No," Jim Luke said, jumping up, "Pa's got ears like a hound dog and can hear a car five miles off. We gotta sneak back in."

Doc said okay, then offered to take Raven Megan home. I suspect she wanted to, but she said, "I have come this far with the gentlemen here, and guess I will go all the way." She smiled when she said it, and it made us feel better.

Jim Luke and I went out the door first and Doc called after us, "Meet me down the trail from your house tomorrow about noon and show me where the body is." Jim Luke nodded and turned away, but before I did I saw the doc lean over and kiss Raven Megan right smack on the lips.

"That's for helping me when I needed you tonight," he said.

Raven Megan looked a little startled, but not mad, like she expected it in a way. I wondered just how well they already knew each other, and felt a deep, gnawing jealousy toward him. My heart went to my toes, and I suddenly hoped that Doc was the killer. I couldn't stay mad long though because Raven Megan seemed so happy to be out with us. She hummed and sang little pieces of songs all the way home.

The sky was growing light in the east when me and Jim Luke slipped through the window. The last thing I remember after slipping into the bed was Jim Luke muttering, "Lord a mighty, with your big mouth there's gonna be so many people lookin' for the killer that even the killer's gonna be helpin' us. Wouldn't surprise me none iffen the dead man climbed right out of the tree and started lookin' hisself."

I was too sleepy to say anything, but I thought all the same that Jim Luke would sure be surprised if that dead man climbed out of that tree. Yes sir, that old Jim Luke would sure be surprised.

CHAPTER 6

It seemed that I'd no more than closed my eyes when Grandpa yelled us out saying we'd better get to jumping if we were going to get Ed Watson's pond cleaned out. Jim Luke groaned. He knew as well as I did that we had no intention of cleaning out that pond. It was our excuse to be free to look for the killer. Of course, we always needed the water before spring rains came. Maybe we could do enough work to make Grandpa think we were working on it. Grandpa said at breakfast that he would do all our chores so we could get an early start.

Jim Luke said he reckoned it would take all day.

Then Grandma said, "You boys better put on your oldest pants, and I'll fix you somethin' to eat there at noon 'stead of havin' to walk all the way home."

"Grandma," I spoke up, "can't you please fix us somethin' 'sides old Bessy?"

Grandma looked sort of startled. "Why, boy, I thought you liked side meat."

"I do, Grandma, but not when it's been named."

She smiled. "All right, I'll fix you some eggs and you can scamper down to the cellar and get some tomatoes to go with them. Mind you, get the ripest ones afore they spoil."

I helped Grandma stuff a sackful of boiled eggs and tomatoes, then wrapped some salt in a corner of paper with some chunks of last night's corn bread.

Jim Luke called the dogs and begged Grandpa for the

twenty-two in case we saw some squirrels. By the time I got my britches on Grandpa had given in, and Jim Luke filled one of his pockets full of shells.

The sun was nearly up to the treetops when we got started. But it had melted almost all the frost off, except in some places it was still sending up whiffs of steam.

The path to the pond was just a cattle trail, almost grown over with weeds. We had to step high and watch for snakes coming out to warm themselves before hibernating for the winter. The dogs were a big help because if there were any around they nearly always sniffed them out in the open before we got there. They always ran ahead of us.

About a mile from the pond old Pepper flushed out a good-sized copperhead, and Jim Luke shot it. He peeled it with his pocketknife and hung the skin on a limb to dry so he could make a hatband. I bet that Jim Luke had peeled fifty snakes since I had been living with him, always going to make him a hatband, and always forgetting about the skins when they were dry.

He was still mad at me for blabbing to the doc, and he wasn't talking to me. But he sure told old Salt what he thought of people he could spit on who went around telling what they weren't supposed to tell. I just ignored him the best I could and whistled like I didn't hear.

When we got to the pond we took a look at the murky, scummy water, stashed the lunch bag high in a tree so nothing could get it, and left the twenty-two there. We then cut north through the woods to meet Doc by the tree. Jim Luke stumped his big toenail nearly clean off, and hobbled all the way snarling, "Shoot fire, shoot fire." I didn't feel sorry for him because of the way he had talked about me to a dog, and just went on as fast as I could, leaving him to limp along the best he could.

Doc was already at the tree. He had climbed on it and was looking down at the dead man inside saying, "Hum, hum, hum, yes, I see." When he saw us he climbed down and said, "Yes sir, there's a dead man in there all right," as if we weren't sure about it. He had his pickup, an ax and a tarp, and said he would get the man out, wrap him in the tarp and take him back to the lab. Then he would find out what had killed him.

I said that in that case I reckoned he could take care of things just fine by himself, for if me and Jim Luke didn't get that pond cleaned out Grandpa would kill us.

For once Jim Luke nodded his head in agreement. He didn't want to be around any more than me when that dead man came out of the tree. Neither did Raven Megan.

She said in a small voice, "I think I will help the boys, Jason."

"Doc laughed. "Come by tonight," he said, "and I'll tell you how he died."

Then he saw Jim Luke's toe and took his black bag from the pickup and poured something from a bottle over it where the nail was cracked. Jim Luke hopped like he had been gut shot. I knew he wanted to cuss but couldn't, as Raven Megan was standing there.

After the doc wrapped a cloth around his toe, Jim Luke tore off down the trail ahead of me and Raven Megan like a turpentined hound. He thought he was far ahead of us but we could still hear "Shoot fire, oh damn, shoot fire" flowing back on the breeze. I started to apologize to Raven Megan, but she sort of listened and giggled. Suddenly it was funny and I laughed too.

When we got back to the pond the dogs were still sitting under the tree where we had left the lunch sack. We decided to eat before we started cleaning the pond. If we didn't do something to it, sure as the world Grandpa would check on it to make sure we did.

We sat on the bank and fed the dogs scraps. I was sure glad we had boiled eggs and fresh tomatoes to offer Raven Megan instead of old Bessy again. She ate almost as much as me and Jim Luke, so we all had to quit just a little hungry. By the time we finished the last bite it was well past noon and the sun was warm like Indian summer. Me and Jim Luke rolled up our pants legs and waded out into the pond, feeling around with our bare toes for sticks and large rocks. When we felt some we plunged our hands down and pulled them up, tossing them far out on the bank. This was to make the water clean for our animals to drink. The water was icy cold at first, but grew warmer as our legs accustomed themselves to the temperature. But nothing could have made the frogs and the tadpoles shooting across our legs and feet feel good. I sure hoped we didn't run into any water moccasins.

Raven Megan watched us for a while and said, "Jim Luke, do you think you ought to be in the water with a sore toe?"

"Oh heck, ma'm," Jim Luke called back, "I been in pond water with lots worse cuts." But his chest swelled out, and the rest of the afternoon he acted like he was doing a job far above and beyond the call of duty, and that the pain was about to kill him but he would keep on or die bravely trying.

Raven Megan watched for a while and looked kind of hesitant, finally took her boots off, pulled up her blue jeans and stepped out into the pond. She sort of gulped, but after a while she started feeling around like we were.

Before long we had the banks of the pond piled with sticks, half-rotten pine cones and some pretty big rocks. Suddenly Raven Megan screamed and jumped as high as she could out of the water. "Somethin' rubbed my foot," she yelled.

Jim Luke got to her first and started laughing. "Why ma'm, I mean, Raven Megan, it's jist an old grandaddy frog."

"Get him away, get him away," Raven Megan yelled, wading as fast as she could for the bank. Jim Luke caught the frog and held him up for Raven Megan to see, but she turned her head, shuddering.

I was about halfway across the pond when my foot hit something hard. I tripped and fell head first into the water. I came up spitting and coughing. When I had caught my breath I reached down to get the thing I had slipped on. When I raised the thing up I just stared, for I held a small gun in my hand. It was thick with mud so I scrubbed at it and dipped it into the water a few times. When I finally cleaned it off it looked almost as good as new.

Splashing through the water I waded to the bank where Raven Megan and Jim Luke were. I yelled, "Hey look, Jim Luke, I found a gun. It must be a toy gun." I was pointing it at them and still talking when Jim Luke and Raven Megan both hit the ground; Jim Luke was yelling "Put that down, Sammy John, don't you point it at us."

It took a few seconds to realize that the gun was real. Then I wanted to throw it away from me, but it had me hypnotized like a cobra does his victim. I managed to point it toward the ground. By the time I reached the bank Jim Luke had his hand held out for it. Without arguing I handed it over. It was a fact, Jim Luke knew more about guns than I did. But as much as he knew, he still couldn't figure out the make of this one.

"I bet that's the gun that killed the man in the tree," Raven Megan said.

"We don't know whether he was shot or not," Jim Luke protested.

"Well, Jim Luke, it stands to reason. Why should someone throw the gun in the pond if it hadn't been used for something it shouldn't have," Raven Megan insisted.

"I think Raven Megan's right," I spoke up, a little hurt that I hadn't gotten more attention and praise for finding it.

"Well, maybe," Jim Luke said doubtfully.

"I'll tell you what," said Raven Megan, "I'll take the gun to Jason and if it's not the gun that killed the man in the tree, you gentlemen can have it back. Does that suit you both?"

We both said yes, but Jim Luke sounded a little doubtful. Raven Megan put on her boots and rolled her pants legs down and took the trail toward Doc's. Me and Jim Luke headed toward some of Grandma's pinto beans, fried potatoes and corn bread. The dogs had long since gone home, not caring much for water.

CHAPTER 7

I was so hungry it took a spell to realize Grandpa and Grandma weren't talking much at supper. Then when I looked up from my plate Jim Luke was sitting kind of stiff and eying them weirdly. I felt my heart go plop, clear to my toes. The first thing I thought was that Doc had told about the dead man, but couldn't bring myself to doubt him long. Still, it wasn't like Grandpa not to ask how the pond cleaning went, or for Grandma to sit there and just keep pushing more beans and potatoes at us.

"Grandpa, we cleaned the pond pretty good," I blurted.

"Fine, fine," said Grandpa, but I could tell his mind wasn't on it.

Jim Luke's Adam's apple bobbed nine to a dozen and he spoke up fast. "Old Salt flushed the purtiest copperhead you ever did see, Pa. I peeled the rascal and soon's the skin's dry I'm gonna make you one of the best hatbands you ever had." Grandpa just nodded absently. It was no use. I couldn't eat any more, nor could Jim Luke. For once Grandma didn't even notice, she was just sitting silently, not eating.

The setting sun bathed the kitchen through the west window, and it would have been the warmest, coziest part of the day except for the tension in us.

Then Grandpa spoke gently, "Sammy, we got a letter from your ma today." I knew from the way he spoke it wasn't an ordinary letter, and had to swallow a few times before speaking. Then it just gushed out.

"She ain't dead like Pa, is she Grandpa?" I queried.

"No, boy, else how could we get a letter from her?"

"Tell me, Grandpa, what's the matter?"

"Well son, your ma's wed again; a city feller."

I sat stunned. I couldn't believe it. It was a while before I could talk again, then I couldn't help asking, "Are they comin' to get me, Grandpa?"

Very gently Grandpa said, "Well, not for a while, Sammy, you see, you ma is gonna have another young'n. Maybe after she gets to feelin' good again, after the young'n comes, she'll come and get you." But I knew she wouldn't, I could tell by Grandpa's voice.

Suddenly my belly heaved and I jumped up and ran out the back door, around the cellar and down behind the barn. I threw up the beans and potatoes and noon eggs, and all the old Bessy I had eaten all of my life. When there was nothing else to come up besides guts, I leaned against the barn with sweat pouring down my face, telling myself I wouldn't ever cry again, never as long as I lived.

Jim Luke appeared beside me and for a while he never said a word. When he did they sent me into a mad rage that even outdid the worst I'd ever seen him throw.

"I am miserable, Sammy. And I'd druthered Pa'd found out about the dead man. And 'sides, Sammy, you don't need to feel so bad. When we get the reward money, you can give your ma's new husband money to leave her, then you can live with her again. Don't cry and puke no more, Sammy."

I whirled. "Cry! And puke! Shoot fire Jim Luke, I ain't cryin', I'm sweatin'. Ain't you got sense enough to know when it's blazin' hot? And as for pukin', I reckon you would too if you'd been pizened. I tell you them taters was spoilt!"

"Well, we ate some and we ain't . . ." But Jim Luke trailed off before he could get it said, and in a sort of

60

feeble voice he added, "I reckon ye be right, Sammy, 'cause I feel kinda sickish."

"And what makes you think I would ever want to live with that old ma of mine anyway?" I went right on yelling, "And that damned old city man. And damn you old shoot fire Jim Luke, what makes you think I'd want to live with bawlin' young'ns that was just half me? And I bet you killed that man in the tree yourself. How does that grab you, you old shoot fire Jim Luke?" My voice rose so loud it startled me and I shut up.

"How'd you like to fight?" Jim Luke said softly, and there wasn't anything he could have asked me that I would have liked better. Without a "by your leave" or "excuse me" I flew into him. I socked and punched him and we rolled nearly all over the barnyard. I was bawling and punching, and it wasn't until I was plumb dog tired, so that I couldn't lift my arms any more, that it came to me that Jim Luke hadn't hit me once. He had just let me punch him. That made me madder than ever because I knew as well as Jim Luke that he could have killed me. Then I was too tired to fight any more, so we just laid near the corncrib with Jim Luke sort of holding onto me. When he spoke his voice was the softest I'd ever heard him speak.

"You know, Sammy John, iffen you don't want to use the money for your ma, you can buy a big shiny car and all sorts of things and ride around showing her what she coulda had iffen she had've waited a little longer. Man," his voice rose in excitement, "we can go to the movie pictures every night, and won't the gals' eyes bug, and I bet they couldn't wait for us to spark them."

I didn't care about the girl part, because I couldn't tell much about them, but it made me feel good that for the first time when Jim Luke was talking about girls, he included me. Best of all, he gave me back a reason to live. I wanted that reward money worse now than I had at first, and I wanted it for revenge, pure and simple.

I would buy that city feller away from my ma, and after he left, whistling cheerfully, I would look at my ma sitting and crying and wondering what in the world she was going to do. Of course, by then there would be four or five little ones hanging around her dress tail. Then while she was crying and looking at me pitifully I would whirl around and get into my shiny car, a bright red one, and speed away with her yelling, "Don't go, Sammy John. Please don't go, please wait, Sammy John."

I would stay away for a week or so and let her really worry, then I would fly up in my bright red car and I would unload all kinds of good stuff, like candy and soda pop and chewing gum of all kinds and flavors, and without a word I'd speed away again.

Suddenly, I liked that darn Jim Luke better than anybody else. I had sense enough to know that in a few days he'd remember me pounding him and beat the hell out of me, but for the time being he had given me something to fill up the empty place where my belly ought to have been. Even if it was hate, it was better than nothing at all being there, like when Grandpa told me about the letter.

Me and Jim Luke couldn't look at each other eye to eye the rest of the evening. He and Grandpa milked and did the chores while Grandma made me eat a bowl of cold milk and corn bread. I was so tired I didn't even remember finishing it or going to bed. I had an impression of the others talking in the kitchen, and Jim Luke was saying, "Poor old Sammy John." I pulled the covers up to my ears. That old shoot fire Jim Luke was sure a good buddy to have.

CHAPTER 8

The next morning Jim Luke was his same old self, and even Grandpa and Grandma acted as if nothing had happened. Grandpa said now that all the crops were laid by we could have the next two weeks before school started to hunt and do as we pleased, except for morning and evening chores. Me and Jim Luke both yelled, "Whoopie." While we were forking hay from the loft to old Ned and the cows, Jim Luke said, "Sammy, I been thinkin', maybe we oughta go spy on Julie Ann. And 'cause she's crazy we'd better not take Raven Megan with us."

I protested, "But Jim Luke, Julie Ann's too old a woman to drop a body down a tree. 'Sides, she's just crazy where religion's concerned. And for all I know maybe she ain't crazy at that. Maybe she just believes that way, and we think she's crazy 'cause we live so far away we don't never go to church. Why, Jim Luke, we haven't been to church but once a year since I been here, and that's just at Christmas when a preacher comes to the school."

"Sammy, you're just sayin' that 'cause you're scared to speak against religion of any sort. You know that old woman's as crazy as hell, and I been thinkin'," he peered all around the barn and then leaned close to me and whispered in my ear, "maybe it was the Klan."

I dropped my pitchfork and hissed, "Shut up, Jim Luke! Don't you ever think it, you hear? 'Sides, why'd they do somethin' like that? And do you want to get the hide stripped off'n our backs? Or a cross burned on our yard come night?"

"Heck no, Sammy, you know I was meaning maybe the dead man was a crook of some kind. A Northern crook. And they've done him in. You know they have a way of doin' away with crooks."

I spit, spit as hard as I could in contempt, all I dared show, of the Klan. I thought we would fight again, but this time Jim Luke would probably kill me. We always fought about the whispered Klan because Jim Luke thought of them as night-riding heroes, handing out justice, and had a secret longing to join them. I thought of them as cowards who didn't have nerve enough to do something alone or to face a man decently, and not cover their faces.

When we weren't fighting about it we were wondering and whispering about who we thought might belong. More than once we thought Uncle Shall might, but we knew Grandpa didn't, as he never went out at night. Besides, if he didn't like something he said so right out loud to a body's face. But even he didn't have much to say against the Klan, other than he was against it: he didn't want our barn to burn down some dark night. I knew Jim Luke thought more about riding around in sheets after dark than about killing people. He'd never hurt anybody that couldn't fight back. But the Klan had always been sort of a bugger man to us. In the hills it was just as terrifying to a child to hear, "If you don't be good, the Klan will get you," as it was to hear, "If you don't be good, the devil will get you." We spent many a night planning to track the local Grand Wizard down.

This morning Jim Luke just a sort of sniffed around me like I was a strange dog for a minute, then started talking about how as soon as it was dark we'd go see Julie Ann. He insisted that maybe Julie Ann had done it because she thought the dead man was a devil or something. We weren't in much of a hurry since we had two whole weeks free, but when we thought about the gun that Doc had and how he was going to tell us how the man was killed, we nearly choked old Bessy throwing food at her.

It was still early morning when we stopped for Raven Megan. We had to wait while she put on her blue jeans and what she called walking boots. I thought she looked mighty pretty in the fuzzy red robe she had on when we got there. We ate breakfast with her again. She didn't cook like Grandma, but it was sure good. We had pancakes, maple syrup and sausage that didn't come from old Bessy. I sure did like that sausage.

When she asked if we were still planning to get rich from the reward money, Jim Luke said, "More than ever," and told her about what my ma had done. Then Raven Megan hugged me, and even though I was feeling pretty good up until then, I felt like bawling something fierce. I had to blink hard, and said I had made a mistake with the pepper on the sausage and got some in my eye.

Raven Megan said, "That sure happens a lot, sometimes my eyes are red all day from making a mistake with the pepper." And Jim Luke, not to be outdone, had to tell about nearly going blind from picking pepper out of the garden and forgetting and rubbing his eyes before he washed his hands.

It was late morning before we finally got started for Doc's place. But the long walk was nice. Raven Megan was sort of dumb about the flowers and plants, so what me and Jim Luke didn't know about them we made up, because she didn't know the difference. She sort of stayed close to me, and heck fire, as long as she was around who needed an old ma who married city fellows anyhow.

Doc came out of his laboratory, grinned and winked at me and Jim Luke, and kissed Raven Megan. We didn't feel bad this time; it was sort of cozy, like we were all kissing her. Then we all sat around his table and me and Jim drank sweet coffee and milk out of cups just like Raven Megan and Doc.

Doc's face turned hard and his eyes glinted when Jim Luke asked, "How did the man die, Doc?"

Doc said a little harshly, "He was hanged. But before he was hanged, he had been whipped." Me and Jim Luke shot quick glances at each other. We both knew it had to be the Klan, for they were bad to whip folks. But we didn't want to believe it, so Jim Luke sort of shook his head at me and we both kept quiet. Raven Megan looked as grim as the doc.

"Well," he went on, "there sure must have been a lot of hate in someone to do that to another human being. I've worked around sickness and death for a long time, but I'll tell you right now I don't think I've ever seen anything as brutally cruel as what this man went through."

Raven Megan had tears in her eyes and her lips quivered as she said, "Do you think someone around here did it? I know they are malicious gossips, but I haven't seen anyone I would think capable of cruelty like this. Maybe someone just brought the body here to throw suspicion onto someone else. Maybe the crime was committed a long way from here."

"It's not likely," Doc said, "the body was more likely put there as a warning, or whoever did it might have heard something and just hid it there for the time being. They might have planned to move it later. Now, if that was the case, somebody is looking for that body. I think we ought to call the police in on this right now. Otherwise, all of us are in danger. Besides, I could get into real trouble by hiding the corpse here."

"Oh please, Doc," Jim Luke said, "I don't know what's right to do now, but how is anyone gonna know the body's here iffen none of us blab it? I know you don't like this at all, neither do we, but could you please give us a week to find the killer? Just a week. I promise that's all we'll ask."

"But, Jim Luke," Doc said, "I'm breaking the law by not turning this body over."

"I know, Doc, but nobody's missin' him, 'ceptin' may-

66

be the killer, and me and Sammy here we haven't hardly started our spying. I can't tell you why, but I think if you report this now we'll be in a lot sight more danger than if you keep quiet."

"All right, Jim Luke," Doc said, "but I don't like it. I don't like it at all. You've got one week, and after that no matter how hard you beg me I'm going to report this." We knew by the expression on his face and the tone of his voice that he meant what he said.

Raven Megan called him off so they could talk alone.

I whispered to Jim Luke, "You know as well as me, Jim Luke, it was the Klan."

"Shut up, Sammy John, you know as well as me that the Klan also has some of the lawmen belonging to it," he said sort of scared, and I was too. He went on, "Iffen the doc tells the lawmen, we are in for it sure. We need to find the killer first and the leader of the Klan hereabouts. If we don't get that leader, he's gonna get us for turning that killer in. Like as not, the others won't do a think if that bugger's out of the way. Then we can call the F.B.I, 'cause, man, we ain't gonna take no chances on nobody around here, and we better get Julie Ann spied on as fast as we can and move on. I don't belive it's Julie Ann neither now, but we gotta work hard and fast and not trust nobody but Doc and Raven Megan," Jim Luke finished breathlessly.

We called, "So long" to them, saying that we had to get home and work. Raven Megan said she would stay with Doc a while, and Doc called for us to be careful and keep our mouths shut and eyes peeled. I don't think he trusted our local law either, or he would have gone ahead and reported the murder.

We were a good piece down the road when Jim Luke remembered the gun and ran back to get it. I waited beside the road, and pretty soon he came back carrying the gun proudly. "Hey," he called excitedly, "Doc said it was a twenty-two caliber pistol. It ain't got no shells, but maybe we can get some sometime." Wistfully he handed it to me. "Here, Sammy," he said, "finders keep-ers."

I started to take it, then didn't because Jim Luke liked guns a lot better than I did. Besides, I'd have given him almost anything after what he'd done for me the day before. And when I said, "Aw, you can have the durn thing, Jim Luke," his face lit up bright, his green eyes danced and he rubbed the gun lovingly.

All he could say as we walked down the road was, "Oh shoot fire, Sammy, shoot fire." But he said it real friendly like, not like when he was whopped or hurt.

It was good dark by the time we got to Julie Ann's, and we had to stop and rest a while near her barn. She lived on a high hill a few miles above Raven Megan. It was one of the steepest hills around, and we were sweat-ing in the cool air by the time we reached the top. When we sat down, panting like dogs, Jim Luke took the gun out of his overall pocket and held it like the gun was a baby.

Tonight was one of Julie Ann's meeting nights. We could hear her warming up. She was sort of a preacher and could see things other folks couldn't, or so she said. Grandpa said he thought she wasn't right in the head. Still, a few old women always came once a week to hear her screech and carry on. We could hear her praying loud and yelling.

Once in a while Jim Luke whispered, "Sammy, she sounds worse than a gut-shot panther."

We waited a little longer in the bushes before sneak-ing up to the window of the front room. We wanted to give all the women who usually came plenty of time to get there. Listening to Julie Ann wasn't anything new for me, and Jim Luke had done it more than once.

We judged the time to be right when we heard her quit praying. There wasn't too much sneaking we had to do, since Julie Ann lived alone and had no dogs to wor-ry about. So we just walked around the barn, across the dusty back yard and around the house right up to the curtainless window, and stood peering into the front room. The room was furnished barely. Mostly it held a lot of chairs, straight and rockers, a few rag rugs faded to not much color at all. She had embroidered "God Bless Our Home" hangings for all four walls. But one thing that was real nice was a great big radio. It was on a table in the middle of the room, pretty and shining as new varnished walnut wood can be. Tonight just Ma Watts and two of her daughters-in-law, Vee and Ruth, were there. But Julie Ann never seemed to care if there were a dozen people or just one. Her sermon never changed either. She always preached the same thing.

Julie Ann was tall and skinny with gray eyes and sort of brown hair which whe wore wrapped around her head in braids. She wore real long dresses that swept the floor. It was hard to tell if she was real old or middle young.

As she warmed up to preach, she would walk and stomp the floor, and before long her dress got sweating wet under the arms and her hair would come down and fall around her face. Sometimes all the women would get to moaning and throwing themselves around. Then it was a sight to see.

Tonight was the same thing, she yelled about a hell of a lot and slung herself around. The women in the chairs rocked and moaned. Always at the end of her yelling, Julie Ann jumped into the middle of the floor and screamed, "The good Lord said in the last days there would be radio, and there it is!"

"Yes, Lord," moaned the women.

Me and Jim Luke usually left after that, but this time when I started backing away Jim Luke nudged me to wait. The women all rose and said, "Thank ya, Sister Julie Ann, your sermon's fine, fine." We hugged the wall until they left. I felt like I was going to break in two all hunkered down the way I was.

The prettiest music brought us straight up with our noses glued to the window. It was music not like a guitar, fiddle or even a banjo. We had never heard a radio play before and it was all lit up. Our eyes popped nearly out, because there was Julie Ann sort of dancing and swaying to the music, her eyes half shut. She was doing it all silently like she was in a trance. She swayed until we thought she would fall over, her back bent so far. And that danged old Julie Ann, we didn't know what to say. Her dress whirled around her knees as she swung around, and her skin looked old and wrinkled. It seemed a shame to look at her as she laughed and twirled around the room.

I quit watching and kept prying Jim Luke until he turned away. We started back down the hill, not saying a word, except Jim Luke kept muttering, "Well, I'll be a dog-eared son of a gun." He said it for a long time, and without saying it to each other, we both knew neither of us would ever tell what we had seen.

CHAPTER 9

We were halfway down the hill when we saw the glow. Jim Luke saw it first and yelled, "Hell fire, Sammy. Raven Megan's house must be afire," and he started running. I looked to where he pointed and sure enough a reddish-white glow came up the hill in back of some trees. With heart pounding, I flew after Jim Luke.

We dashed down the hill and tore over rocks and jumped fallen trees in the strip of woods. We burst through the trees in front of Raven Megan's house and stopped as suddenly as if we had run into a wall. Our bodies stiffened, filled with horror, for on Raven Megan's yard the cross of the K.K.K. burned, glowing down to red hot coals.

For a minute I thought Raven Megan was screaming until I realized Jim Luke was yelling, "Fire!" over and over. We ran, skirting the hot coal, realizing there was no danger to us because the Klan had done its work and disappeared into the dark. But we felt fear for Raven Megan.

We didn't stop to knock. The door opened under Jim Luke's push, and we were in the house. Raven Megan sat on the couch, holding something in her hand, dumbly staring at it. Wind blew the curtains behind the couch where she sat, through a broken window pane. Raven Megan didn't even raise her head. Me on one side and Jim Luke on the other, we put our arms across her shoulders.

"Raven Megan, Raven Megan, are you hurt? Please, Raven Megan, talk to us. Be ye hurt?" I asked.

Dazedly she raised her head and looked at us, and without a word she started shivering and jerking.

"I'm gonna go get Doc," Jim Luke yelled, "stay with her, Sammy. Lock the door and don't let nobody in 'til I come and tell you to."

"We'll be all right, Jim Luke, but hurry," I said. He flew like a streak of light. Before I even had the door locked and the windows closed his beating footsteps had faded down the road toward Doc's.

Raven Megan was still just sitting there. I knelt beside her, "Please, Raven Megan, be ye all right? I'll take good care of you. Please be all right," I said, and talked to her over and over, but she didn't seem to hear me, she just kept jerking and shaking. I wished fiercely that I had some of Grandpa's medicine to give her. I was afraid to go look for anything anyplace and leave her alone. I did leave her long enough to build a fire in the fireplace and one in the kitchen stove. Then I put some water in the coffeepot to boil. I didn't know how to make coffee, but figured on having hot water when Doc came so he could.

There was one of the prettiest chocolate cakes I had ever seen sitting on the kitchen table, and I couldn't help taking a swipe at it with my finger and getting a small taste.

I lit some more coal oil lamps, then not knowing just what else to do, I just sat and put my hand on Raven Megan's head. Her hair felt soft as silk, so I sort of rubbed it. Once in a while I asked her to talk and if she was hurt. I had never seen anything shake like she was since old Salt had a running fit, and once when he had worms.

I wondered what the paper she had in her hand was, but she wouldn't let go of it. I got up and moved the water back on the kitchen stove where it would stay hot without boiling over, and took another log and put it on the fireplace. I was beginning to think Jim Luke had been caught by the Klan or that Doc hadn't been home when I heard a car screeching up and gravel spinning. My heart nearly choked me until I heard Jim Luke holler, "Open up, Sammy John."

I flew to the door and Doc went right past, nearly knocking me and Jim Luke both down, rushing to the couch where Raven Megan lay. Me and Jim Luke crowded around him as he tilted her head and lifted her eyelids with his finger. He muttered something about shock and took a needle and something else from his black bag. After sticking the needle in a little bottle, he gave her a shot.

He held her for a while, sort of rocking and cussing, and then he snapped, "Get a blanket."

It took me and Jim Luke a while to find one. Then we had to pull it off the bed because we didn't know where Raven Megan kept things. Doc propped her head on a pillow and covered her with the blanket.

After taking the paper from her hand, he read it and his face became dark like thunder. Then he threw it toward the fireplace, but it landed on the floor in front of it.

When he went to the kitchen I followed him and told him he'd better make coffee while the water was hot since I didn't know how. He made it and gave me and Jim Luke a cup, not even remembering to put mostly milk and sugar in it this time. It didn't taste so good, but we acted as if we liked it, and me and Jim Luke ate some of the cake.

Doc raised Raven Megan's head and poured some coffee into her mouth. She rolled around and talked sleepy like, and when Doc asked her what happened she told him without shaking or acting like she was upset— just like she wanted to get through and go back to sleep.

"I had finished baking a cake this evening," she said, "in case my gentlemen companions came around again tomorrow." She sort of half grinned at me and Jim Luke and went on, "When I heard a noise like the front gate opening, I went to the front room and looked. My hair nearly stood on end, for slipping through the gate were a dozen or more men. I thought at first they were ghosts, but you know I don't really believe in ghosts. But, Jason, when it finally came to me what they were it scared me worse than if they had been ghosts. Before I could scream or anything they put down the cross that two of them had been carrying, then one poured something on it and set it on fire. Oh, it was awful. They wore sheets with hoods that had eye holes in them. When the cross was burning good they called filthy names toward the house. I thought they would never stop. Just when I thought I'd faint, they started to leave, but just before they did one of them threw a rock through the window, barely missing me, and it had a note around it. It said, never mind . . ." her voice trailed off.

"I know what it said," Doc said gently. "Go to sleep now." Her eyes closed and Doc turned to us and said, "You men better go home now, your grandparents will be worried. But I can never thank you enough for what you've done." Solemnly he shook hands with us. We sort of hesitated about leaving, but Doc said kindly, "Don't worry, I'll stay the night and take care of her. You men come and take over tomorrow, all right?"

"Sure, fine, yes, Doc, we'll take over," we answered, proudly and bravely. It wasn't until we were through the orchard and near the house that Jim Luke showed me the note he had picked up by Raven Megan's fireplace where Doc had thrown it. In the moonlight the printed words stood out plain and black. There were only three words, "Whore of Babylon."

I felt sick with rage. Raven Megan was no more a whore than me or Jim Luke. Not even Jim Luke would do anything really bad, even though he had always been a bit earthy.

Jim Luke hissed over and over through his clenched teeth, "Shoot fire, shoot fire," and kept it up all night, even after we went to bed. Now and then I joined him, but underneath, for the first time, lay real fear, stark, naked, raw fear. Only people raised in the South can

74

know the real meaning of the Klan. Nearly paralyzed with fear, we made a pact between us to find out who was the leader and who the members were.

No matter where my thoughts turned, they always came back to Uncle Shall, because he hardly ever worked, and we had heard Aunt Imie tell Grandma and my aunts how much Uncle Shall worried her staying out nights. She said sometimes he didn't come home until near sunup. It was sure scary thinking that maybe one of our kin could be a member of the Klan, or maybe even the leader of the mysterious hill Klan. Somehow it didn't seem possible that anybody we knew could kill or whip or burn other folks' things.

We went to sleep swearing not to sleep again until we had spied on all the folks we knew, kin or not, at least until school started.

CHAPTER 10

When we woke, it was later than usual and we remembered it was our free time before school started. Jim Luke burned the message the Klan had thrown through Raven Megan's window. We didn't take much time to eat breakfast, just fed the animals fast and ducked through the orchard toward Raven Megan's.

She opened the door, looking prettier than usual, and like nothing at all had happened. Doc yelled from the kitchen, "Come on in, boys, and eat with us." On the way to the kitchen Raven Megan kept saying how brave me and Jim Luke were and how proud she was to have us for friends, and how brave we were to help her the night before. It was plumb shaming, and made a body wish she would hush and never stop saying it at the same time.

Neither Jim Luke or I said we'd already eaten, because Raven Megan's food sure looked good. Besides, there was more than half of that chocolate cake left and Doc always gave us coffee. Nobody talked much at first. We ate eggs, bacon and toast, but nobody said anything about the cake, so I decided to stare at it hard until Raven Megan noticed. I stared and stared, almost able to taste the rich chocolate with the icing running all gooey down my throat.

Doc brought our coffee. This time he remembered to make it mostly milk. I looked up to see why Raven Megan wasn't noticing me staring at the cake, and I saw she was too busy staring at Doc and him at her. I caught Jim Luke's eye and nodded at the cake so he started staring at it too. We stared and stared, because Grandma had always told us not to ask first, but wait until it was offered.

I was beginning to give up on the cake when Doc laughed outright with the biggest laugh I had ever heard from him. But me and Jim Luke were afraid to look away from the cake. Then Raven Megan started giggling. I decided to give up on the cake and see what was gong on, but just then Raven Megan said, "Oh my, I don't know what has gotten into me, I was planning to have that cake for breakfast and just about forgot it. Would you gentlemen please forgive me?" So saying, she reached for a knife and cut huge pieces and laid them on our plates. Then she and Doc took little pieces. But I would have forgiven her anything; she had a right to forget the cake after all she had been through the night before, and for all the goo running down my throat I would have given her old Salt and sold Jim Luke into slavery.

Jim Luke's big ears were flopping from pure joy as he chewed and swallowed. I didn't even feel a pang at thinking of selling him, because nobody on God's green earth had a right to cook such good cake and be as pretty as that Raven Megan. I made up my mind to ask Doc to marry her so she would always be around since me and Jim Luke were too young to do it.

Before I could say anything, Jim Luke swallowed the last of his cake and started talking, "Doc," he said, "are you gonna turn in the Klan for what they done last night to Raven Megan, and for killing that man in the tree?" Raven Megan turned kind of pale and Doc's face went hard and wasn't friendly at all.

"Hell no, Jim Luke," he said, "you know as well as I that the sheriff could very well be the leader of the skunk Klan, the dirty sons of bitches; picking on helpless women. This secret of ours must stay ours too. And, boys, whatever you do, don't trust, and I repeat, don't trust or tell anyone. Now this raid here last night didn't have anything to do with the murder. They did this because Raven Megan wouldn't have anything to do with the pawing maniacs, and what's more, I'll be here or she's going to be with me and I will blow their damn fool heads off if they mess with me. And, boys, I want your promise, if anything happens you will protect her and hide her if necessary until help comes. Promise?"

"Sir, I give you my word that me and Sammy John will guard Raven Megan with our lives," Jim Luke said solemnly and grownup like. He and Doc shook hands. I gulped and Raven Megan cried a little, then Doc shook hands with me, and kissed Raven Megan. Then me and Jim Luke kissed her, and it was sort of nice so Jim Luke kissed her again, but the third time Doc said, "Whoa there," and pulled him back. Then Raven Megan and Doc laughed.

Before we left to get on with our spying, Doc said he was going to town and was taking Raven Megan with him. He was going to contact the F.B.I because the local law was no good. That was no news to me and Jim Luke. But he told us not to worry, that we still had time to find the killer, or more likely, killers; and he told us to be sure to watch out for ourselves, and whatever we did to be quiet about it.

When we got outside Jim Luke said, "Sammy, we gotta figure out a way to get Uncle Shall to own up to belongin' to the Klan without him knowing it's us." I felt sad thinking about all the fishing trips we had been on with him, then hardened myself because anybody that would do something to a girl was rotten to the core. And anybody that would whip a man before killing him was sick in the mind, and the only thing I could think of that was that rotten was the Klan. Even Grandpa said they were rotten, but they were sure as hell a scary, rotten bunch, and it was no shame to feel afraid because even grown-up men were.

"Come on, Sammy," Jim Luke said, "let's go sit by the spring and think on it. They's gotta be a way." But before we got to the spring Jim Luke whispered, "Hey, Sammy John, we will do him like they done Raven Megan. We'll burn a cross on his yard and then throw a note through the window saying the body's been found. That ought to put a cuckleburr up his hind end and send him flying to the rest of them. Leastways we'll know whether he belongs or not."

We got busy night and day making a cross out of pine because it always burned good. When we had it tied in a cross, Jim Luke snuck the coal oil out of the lamp and soaked the wood. I pretended I wanted some corn bread out of the warming oven, and when Grandma's head was turned I grabbed some matches. Since Jim Luke wrote better than me, he printed "The body has been found" on some brown wrapping paper, and tied it around a rock and put it in his pocket.

The darker it got the more scared we became, because messing with the Klan was worse than having a dead hand grab a person. We huddled closer together, and when I said I didn't want any supper Jim Luke said I'd better eat all I could hold since we might have a lot of running to do before the night was over. Then he said, "Sammy, iffen they get after us and we get separated, you just keep a goin' north."

"What about you?" I whispered, more scared than ever.

"Don't worry, Sammy. I'll be over the line before you." And I knew if he was ever telling the truth it was now, because boy, that old Jim Luke didn't mess around any, when he got scared he ran. During supper I watched him like a hawk, and everything he ate I ate more of, because if there was any running to do this was one time I was determined to outrun that old shoot fire Jim Luke or die trying.

It seemed like even the good old moon had gone back on us. For the last week it had been fat and yellow white, and it was now just a pale slit. The darkness under the trees was so dense that a body could choke on it. Even in open places the darkness was just a hair lighter.

It was a good five miles to Uncle Shall's, as the crow flies, and that was the way we were going, the way the crow went, cutting through hollows and climbing hills, tripping over fallen logs and knocking our toenails off on rocks. It was too dark to see.

We didn't dare to go over the road like we usually did because who knew what might be out riding on a night like this. I shivered and hung onto Jim Luke's shirttail, and it wouldn't have surprised me if we stepped into a bed of rattlesnakes before long. At least that would keep us from falling into the hands of the Klan. I shuddered away from the thought and just tried to keep my mind on hanging onto Jim Luke.

I don't think I really came to my senses until we were laboring up the last hill, with Jim Luke gasping, "Shoot fire, Sammy John, it's hard enough to climb this hill without having to drag you too." I realized that I had just been hanging on mostly and letting him do most of the work. I turned loose before he could knock me off and started walking.

Between the trees we could see a light shining through a window. I was glad Uncle Shall's dogs knew us. Jim Luke was still saying, "Shoot fire, Sammy, I can't hardly breathe, dragging this cross and you too. Like one wasn't enough. Iffen I had enough breath I'd whop you a good one. What in the cat hair ye think I be, a mule?"

"I'm sorry, Jim Luke, but you better be quiet. 'Sides, if you whop me, I might holler, and they would hear us."

"Not with my fist down your gullet," Jim Luke kept muttering.

Pretty soon he quit, and we crawled close as we could to the yard. It was easy because the woods grew nearly up to the door. I got sort of scared then, because what if Uncle Shall didn't belong to the Klan after all, and we scared him into having a heart attack or something. I whispered as much to Jim Luke. He whispered back that it was a chance we all had to take, including Uncle Shall, and Jim Juke's sister Imie.

Jim Luke said for me to stay back in the trees and handed me the rock with the note on it to throw as soon as he set the match to the cross.

While he crawled up with the cross, placing it as near to the door as he could, I measured the distance from where I stood to the window with the lamp in it, swinging my throwing arm to loosen it up. When I saw the flicker of a match out of the corner of my eye, I got up and let fly with the rock.

The cross seemed to leap into flames just as there was the sound of breaking glass and Aunt Imie's high, shrill screams. I just stood staring until Jim Luke came flying up and screamed as loud as he could whisper, "Climb a tree, ya dad-blamed idiot." And when he went up a huge acorn tree I was hot on his heels, in fact I almost pulled him down when I reached up for a limb to pull myself up, and got his foot instead. He almost kicked my brains out before I let go.

We peered down from the very top of the tree. Uncle Shall had come out the door and was peering everywhere with his shotgun in his hands, and I was praying he wouldn't look up. We could see him as plain as could be. I wished to hell Aunt Imie would shut up screaming, even the young ones were beginning to yell. I hung onto the tree hard as I could, and hooked my legs around the trunk in case I fainted so I wouldn't fall. I figured that if fear didn't get me the smell would. I could smell Jim Luke's foot hanging close to my nose, and he had stepped on something that stunk like a barn stall.

Uncle Shall started toward his truck and Aunt Imie was standing in the door with a child on each hip, yelling at him. I couldn't make out what she was yelling to him, but heard Uncle Shall answer her as he looked over his shoulder. He said, "Well, it scared the hell out of me too. But I still gotta go get the sheriff."

"Jim Luke," I whispered, "I can't help feeling sorry for Uncle Shall if he does belong to the Klan."

"Aw hell, Sammy," Jim Luke whispered back, "anybody that would be that rotten, kinfolks or not, oughta have somethin' done to them. You know how Uncle Shall likes to talk, and what we done to him will be all over the hills before midnight."

I sighed with relief that I wouldn't have the guilt alone on my conscience for turning on a kinsman.

As soon as Uncle Shall was out of sight, and Aunt Imie had the door shut, and no doubt locked and bolted, we slid down the tree and made our way toward the woods and the rotten, hollow tree below the house. Jim Luke was still sore about pulling me up the hill, and wouldn't talk or wait when I got tangled up in vines or fallen trees.

When we reached the tree where the body had been, we burrowed deep into the undergrowth, far back under a brush pile where we could see all around it, than settled down to wait. Jim Luke swore that if I coughed, sneezed or made any noise at all to give us away, if they let him live, even if he was skinned alive, he would kill me in the most painful way he could think up.

I told him he needn't worry because I figured to die quietly as soon as I saw the Klan coming through the trees. That shut him up and we lay quietly, waiting and waiting. We waited so long that my shaking even stopped. I could feel sweat running down between my shoulder blades, and I had a terrible urge to go to the toilet. I was cold, and my ears, nose and toes felt numb. I felt like if I didn't move or at least twitch, I could die, then felt like I couldn't if my life depended on it because a white shape like a ghost slipped out of the woods near the tree, then another one and another. I could hardly breathe, and they were so near I could have touched them on their feet. There were six of them. They were all white except for black holes where their eyes would have been. They had no eyes, no nose, no mouth or anything. They looked like something evil from hell.

I heard a long whistle. It must have been an all-clear signal, because one of them brought out a small lantern and lit it. In the light they looked more scary than in the dark. They sure looked like they were imps of hell with a reddish glow over the black eye holes.

A little of my fear and stiffness left my body when one of them spoke, for it made them seem more human. The leader's voice was muffled as he held the lantern up high. "One of you boys shinny up the tree and look." One of the figures, smaller than the rest, climbed the tree. The other held the lantern up to the hole in the rotten tree and peered down. "Hell fire," he snapped, "there ain't no body in here." There was quick movement among the hooded figures, and they all crowded around the tree, then tried to stretch their necks and look in. There was mingled cussing in different tones of voice. Some seemed a little shrill from fear, and others just seemed mad. I was more afraid of the scared ones than of the mad ones because Grandpa always said a scared coward was a lot worse and could hurt a body more than the maddest brave man.

Finally the one who had held the lantern said sharply to be quiet, and he said, "Now shut up and think!" They grew quiet. "Now listen, men," he went on, "somebody pulled a fast one on us. We gotta figure what happened, and who has the body now, because if the F.B.I. is called in on this then there's gonna be hell to pay. You know how they've been lately, and some of them have even joined us pretending to be one of us."

"Why would the sons of bitches who did this go to Shall's place?" another voice asked.

"Well, 'cause they had some suspicion that he belongs to us, you damn fool," one of the men answered, "or else the bastard who did it knew good and well that big-mouthed Shall would spread it."

"If I ever catch them I'll take the skin from their backs," piped up one of the men, we couldn't tell who.

I could feel my skin crawl. "Well, spread out men and see if you can find any clues or marks around here," said the leader.

One of the men nearly stepped on my hand. I tried to

squirm my body into the ground. The man with the lantern was holding it close over the road.

They had found the tire tracks of Doc's pickup. There was more muttering and cursing, and one said, "Oh hell, it's too dark to find anything," and the one who spoke walked over and nearly sat on Jim Luke, lifted his hood and lit a cigarette. I stared until my eyes nearly popped out of their sockets, because when the match's glow lit up his face for a minute I knew him. Lord have mercy! It was Rudy Spraddle, that little skinny daddy of all them kids. I almost died on the spot as my heart pounded like crazy. Other men came to sit around and smoke quietly near us and the tree, but it was too dark, or my eyes were blinded by fear, because I couldn't make out their faces. The leader had blown out the lantern.

They smoked for a while, then after pulling his hood down and stomping on the glowing end of his cigarette, the leader said, "Well, men, we've got our work cut out for us. I reckon the Grand Wizard ought to know what happened, and we should get his advice on whether or not to go ahead and find the stinking bastard that found the body. But I warn you all to keep your lips buttoned tight, 'cause this is liable to get a lot worse before we have heard the last of it. I will meet you all at the Old Turner place at midnight tomorrow, and if the Grand Wizard thinks it's important enough, he might be with me. Now be careful."

There was a gasp when he said the Grand Wizard might come, as if he were the devil himself, and I figured maybe he was.

As for what happened next, I wouldn't have believed it if my own ears and eyes hadn't heard and seen it. Them buggers bowed their heads, and the leader led them in prayer, as if he were a preacher and they were in church. He prayed for success in their work just like Grandpa would pray for rain to make the crops grow. After the leader said a most self-righteous amen, there was a moment of quiet, and darn his hide, that dang Jim

84

Luke sneezed. He sneezed so loud it rang the death knell in my ears.

Slowly, so slowly that the heads of the men looked like scarecrows, they turned toward where we lay. "Did any of you sneeze?" asked the leader. Five voices said no. Suddenly the leader yelled, "Spread around the brush, boys, and don't let him out." My heart thumped to my toes.

The men started running around the brush pile in back of us. I shot out of the front in one movement, and just caught a glance of a shadow out of the corner of my eye. Cursing and yelling, the ghost figures stumbled over the brush after us. We were fast though and my brain kept screaming, north, north, north, to my feet, but my feet flew any way that a path cleared for them.

I heard a thump and a growl like a bunch of wild cats were behind me and a "shoot fire." I knew that Jim Luke had been caught or had fallen in some berry vines. I hoped it was the vines, but wasn't about to stop and see. Instead of stopping me it sped me on, and if Jim Luke didn't make it I could always tell myself later that I was running for help.

I must have run two miles and was slowing a little, thinking I'd better go back, and if there was nothing else I could do I could be killed with Jim Luke. Then near-naked flesh flew past me and hissed, "Run, you damn mule, run!" I needed no further urging. I flew like the wind. When I was near passing out from lack of breath, I came across Jim Luke laying across a log, gasping. Asking no questions then, I laid down and gasped with him.

We had no more than got to breathing easy when we heard them coming again. Jim Luke jumped up, and grabbing my arm he pushed me flat to the ground behind the log. We hardly dared to move. The men were walking slow and talking in low tones in their search for us. The voice I remembered, and now knew to belong to Rudy Spraddle, whined, "You reckon them young'ns will tell? And what about our meeting?"

"Aw hell," came the voice of the leader, "they was just kids out possum huntin' and we scared the hell out'n them. Besides, they were so scared they will be hiding under the bed for the next two weeks, har, har, har."

I felt Jim Luke go stiff and I held him with all my strength. He must have been kind of weak, because I didn't have much strength left myself. I knew I'd better do something soon, because even though Jim Luke was a little earthy he had a certain brand of dignity, and when anyone made fun of it, he was ready to fight. I knew he hated those men for seeing him go through the briar patch on all fours.

The men went out of hearing range, and when I raised my head above the bushes they were out of sight, too. We stumbled toward home so tired we could hardly walk. Pride kept Jim Luke going, but just plain fear made my feet move when my body quit.

The sun was coming up as we made the last lap up the hill. I was shivering from the aftermath of our run and from being cold, and Jim Luke looked blue because he was as close to being naked as could be with just tatters of his britches and just the neck and cuffs of his shirt left.

Grandma was standing on the porch shading her eyes with her hand when she saw Jim Luke. We could hear her calling, "Mercy, mercy." Grandpa walked around the corner of the house and walked down the road to meet us. Before he could say a word, Jim Luke spit out of the corner of his mouth and walked up to Grandpa, looking him straight in the eye, and he said, "Pa, you won't ever believe this, but I got tangled up in a roll of barbed wire over nigh Sam Baker's place and it took Sammy John nigh all night to get me out of there."

Grandpa sort of squinted his eyes and the corners of his mouth quirked. "Well, son," he drawled, "I reckon seein' is believin'." He looked at Jim Luke from head to toe, and without another word he whistled for old Salt and Pepper and went off across the pasture. Jim Luke told the same story to Grandma, who said, "Mercy,

mercy," again and found him some more overalls to put on.

We fell across the bed, hungry but too tired to get up and eat.

"Sammy," Jim Luke whispered just before he fell asleep, "it's the Grand Wizard we gotta catch, that bastard is the one who gives the orders and is the real killer."

"Oh, Jim Luke," I said, "I just remembered something. The man that nigh sat on you to smoke was Rudy Spraddle. I seen his face when he lit a cigarette."

"Well, we'll get that dad-blamed little runt, too," Jim Luke said, and closed his eyes.

CHAPTER 11

It was near sundown when Grandpa woke us with, "Supper's ready!" Lord, it didn't seem like I could eat fast enough. I felt empty clear to my toes.

Jim Luke asked Grandpa if we could have some of the traps from the barn so we could set them for possums. He made his voice excited and said, "We might even get a coon." I tried to look as excited as Jim Luke. Grandpa smiled his "ain't it nice to be kids" at Grandma, and told us to go ahead, but try to get back before sunup this time.

As soon as we finished, we tore out to the barn, and while Jim Luke oiled the traps and made sure they worked, I did the chores. The traps were old, but in good shape. They were steel and big enough to break a man's leg.

"What're we gonna do with them traps, Jim Luke?" I asked as we threw them over our shoulders and started down the hill. "And where are we going?" I asked.

"First we're goin' to see Doc," said Jim Luke, "then we're gonna go to the old Turner place. While the Klan's meetin' we're gonna set the traps around the place, by crackety, and we're gonna catch us some K.K.K. Well, four anyhow, 'cause that's all the traps we have, and when they go to Doc's to get their chewed-up legs fixed, Doc will know who they are." Jim Luke sniggered. Boy! That dad-blamed Jim Luke was sure smart, and we knew every foot of the old Turner place. It had been deserted for years and we often played and hunted there.

We went to Raven Megan's first, but nobody was around, so we headed for Doc's. They were in the laboratory. Raven Megan was holding rabbits for Doc to shoot full of stuff. When we told the story of the night before and why we had the traps, Raven Megan started crying again and Doc kept slapping our shoulders and saying, "Well I'll be damned."

Finally when we had quieted down, he told us, "I contacted the F.B.I., and a man will be here in three days from Washington. I tell you, I'm worried about you boys going around that Klan. You were lucky last night, they didn't recognize you, but no telling what they will do if they catch you at the Turner place."

Raven Megan said, "Don't you think you ought to wait and just tell the man from the F.B.I. what you know? Please don't put yourselves into a dangerous predicament when you don't have to, it's not worth it."

"Well," Jim Luke said, "you've got a point all right, Raven Megan, but," then he turned to Doc, "Doc, don't you see why we have to do it? Have you thought of a better plan?"

"No, Jim Luke," Doc said, "I can't think of any way to beat your plan, and if you have to go through with it promise me you won't show yourselves."

"Okay, Doc," Jim Luke said, "we'll be real careful." We shook hands with Doc and kissed Raven Megan, then left.

An unspoken code of the hills is to take care of your own. That means from protecting them to punishing them. If your own son committed a crime, you would be responsible for whatever his punishment consisted of, be it simple or be it an eye for an eye. No outsider is welcomed in a case like that. So we hadn't told about Rudy Spraddle being one of the Klan because like other hill men we believed in taking care of our own and punishing them. In fact I grumbled to Jim Luke that it looked like all the Klan might be our own hill folks. Even though we liked Doc a lot and loved Raven Megan, we still considered them outsiders in a way.

We had until midnight, so we headed for the Spraddle place. Jim Luke looked so wicked it nearly scared me, and I knew he was thinking of the briar patch, and I felt a little sorry for Rudy Spraddle. I told Jim Luke so.

"Hell," Jim Luke said, "I ain't sorry for the little chicken runt coward. Do you reckon he felt sorry for the man they whopped and killed? Sammy John, you know as well as me that Pa allus said it was better to kill a grown man than for another man to whop him. It's not like fist fightin', Sammy, but like bein' tied up and whopped like an animal. I don't feel sorry for nobody that would do that, and for the whole bunch to gang up on one man, Sammy, that's just too much for my craw to hold."

"You know, Jim Luke, I allus thought you wanted to join the Klan," I said curiously. "What changed your mind?"

"Sammy, I never did really, I just say things sometimes to get under Pa's skin. Course then, too, I thought it would be excitin' for a while, but whippin' people and playin' God almighty ain't for me or no human to do," he said.

"I'm glad to hear you say that, Jim Luke," I said, and sort of punched him on the shoulder. We got quiet then as we got close to the Spraddle place.

"Sammy," he said, "let's put the traps nigh the road and slip out to the back of the house. Afore long Rudy will come out to go to the meetin' of the Klan and we'll sore scare the britches clean off'n him. Let's get him down by the creek, and as ghost-like as you can, say, 'I'm the man from the tree and I have come to take you with me.' There's just a narrow path there and he'll have to run, and I'll block the other end and say the same thing when he gets to me."

"Okay, Jim Luke," I said. I started giggling, because

90

I knew what Jim Luke had in mind. There was nothing on each side of the path except blackberry vines with thorns by the thousands.

"Shhhh," Jim Luke said, and we laid the traps beside the road and crept around the house to watch the back door where the path led to the creek. We figured he would go out that way because the old Turner place was across the creek in an open field about five miles over the creek bottom land. Besides, if someone were to be passing, Rudy wouldn't want to be seen out that late at night.

Jim Luke whispered, "Sammy, go about twenty yards from the house and let him pass you afore ye speak, and be sure you be in back of him so's he can't bolt for the house. I'm goin' down further so I can speak in front of him." Jim Luke slipped away and I crept further down the path and stood against a tree looking at the back door of the house.

The moon was still a slit, but the stars were a sparkling blanket overhead. At a squeaking noise I yanked my gaze away from them to the back door of the house in time to see Rudy slip through a gleam of light, carrying a bundle under his arm. I sunk into the shadows of the tree and glued my ears to the sound of his footsteps on the sandy creek bottom path. I tried to silently clear my throat a few times and swallowed a few times. I let him get about ten feet in front of me then stepped out, blocking the path back to the house.

As deep as I could I said, "Rudy Spraddle." He jumped about four feet off the ground, then froze stiff as a dog pointing birds. "I am the man from the tree and I have come to get you." My voice went squeaky at the end, but I think Rudy was past hearing me.

I was beginning to think we had gone too far and had scared him to death when he screamed, "Lordy, Lordy," and started running. He had only gone a few leaping steps when he came to a screeching halt. Then I heard Jim Luke's voice saying the same thing I had. It sound-

ed so low and ghost like that I nearly ran off. With one
ghost in back and one in front, it was too much for the
cowardly Rudy. He stepped sideways and dropped the
bundle he carried, then tore out through the blackberry
vines screaming every step of the way. He probably
thought every time he got snagged on a thorn that the
ghost had hold of him. For the first time I felt I was paid
back for the dead hand holding me. It served that dang
Rudy right, and I laid down on the path and rolled,
laughing fit to kill, and Jim Luke did too. We both burst
out laughing again when we heard Rudy go through the
vines and hit the cold creek water with a yelp. We knew
the vines had picked him nearly as clean as they had
Jim Luke, and hitting cold creek water on top of everything else was more than we had hoped for.

We came to our senses slowly, leaning on each other
and gasping, with tears running down our faces. When
we could catch our breath Jim Luke jumped up and
said, "We gotta hurry, Sammy John, let's get the traps."

He turned to go and stumped his toe on the bundle
Rudy had dropped. He lifted it and it came unrolled. It
was the costume of the Klan.

I didn't like the way Jim Luke was fingering it, and
without his saying a word I said, "No sir, Jim Luke, you
can't do it! No, Jim Luke, they'd find out and kill you.
Besides you don't know the password."

"Sammy," Jim Luke said in a voice that meant no
back talk, "I am the same size as Rudy, and iffen we get
there first I won't need no password, and I'll be the only
one that knows where the traps are. In the excitement of
the others getting caught, I'll run off. Just think, Sammy, I might find out who the Grand Wizard is." His
voice lifted with pure greed and excitement.

"But listen, Jim Luke," I protested, knowing dang
good and well it would do no good, "they allus keep
their heads covered."

"Aw hell, Sammy, I know that, but you know they're
bound to know each other. 'Sides, remember how they

92

smoked last night? Don't worry, Sammy, and come on. We got to get movin' if we are goin' to get there afore them," he said, moving toward the traps carrying the bundle.

CHAPTER 12

It was almost midnight by the time we got to the old Turner place. At least I felt in my bones it was. Jim Luke stopped and pulled the hood and sheet over himself, giving me instructions in a low voice.

"Sammy, set the traps in front of the doorstep, just as soon as everybody is in the cabin. And when we come out I will step off'n to one side and run."

"If you come out!" I said mean like. But Jim Luke just poked me on the shoulder and got down on his knees and helped me spring the traps so all I would have to do was ease them in place one at a time.

The old Turner house was nearly falling down after being unoccupied for so long, and there were loose bricks from the chimney laying all over the ground. Jim Luke told me to take the traps into the lilac bushes near the falling chimney and window, then he told me when the meeting got going good to crawl out with one trap at a time and put them in front of the doorstep. He said not to make any noise or catch myself in one of the traps.

Then he said, "When you see me, start runnin'. You better fly right after me," he hissed, and after thumping me on the shoulder again he went around the corner to sit on the steps and wait.

I lay still, listening for footsteps. I felt a bug crawling up my britches leg and nearly went crazy until I rubbed my leg on the ground as hard as I could and squashed it.

"Hey," Jim Luke whispered around the corner, "I'm gonna try and pull the Grand Wizard's hood off. After you set the traps, look in the winder and try to get a good look at him."

"You can't, Jim Luke. Oh please, Jim Luke, you can't do that." I couldn't help it, I was nearly crying. "Iffen you do, I'll tell Grandpa."

"Shut up, Sammy," Jim Luke hissed, "somebody's comin'." Then I did cry, but managed to stifle it. Sure as the world that dang Jim Luke was going to get us killed. I even wished I was with my ma, city husband and all.

I felt like I had a roaring in my ears, but heard plain enough when Jim Luke spoke in a voice so much like Rudy's it made my hair stand on end.

He said, "Password, brother," and the voice of the slim man who had climbed the tree the night before said, "Defender of the South, Righters of Wrong, Defenders of Southern Womanhood." I couldn't help it, all my crying quit and I thought, oh my hind end, if all the women looked like Rudy Spraddle's wife they didn't need any defending. Oh my hind end. I nearly sniggered out loud, and wondered how in the cat hair Jim Luke could keep a straight face.

There was no sound of laughter, however, when Jim Luke said, solemn like, "Pass, brother." But when the Klansman got in the house and lit a lamp the hair nearly lifted clear off my head, for its rays fell straight across my legs showing them and my bare toes as plain as day. I nearly died trying to double up and wiggle back under the bushes, and all the time Jim Luke was saying, "Password, brother," as the Klan came on.

By the time I got myself out of sight, they were all in the house, including Jim Luke. I tried to pray, but kept wondering what was going on. So I sneaked around and crawled until I had slowly moved all the traps, one at a time in front of the doorstep. I thought I would die because my heart pounded so with relief when I put the last one in place, and I eased up to the window to peer in. Some of the windowpanes were broken out, so it was

95

easy to hear. But what made my eyes pop out was Jim Luke standing near the door with the big man, the leader of the night before. And with him was an even taller man. Jim Luke would need a ladder to yank his hood off. Around a rickety table with an oil lamp in the center, sat the other men of the Klan.

I felt around on the ground with my toe until I found one of the loose chimney bricks, and eased down until I had it in my hand. I had a vague idea that if they caught Jim Luke I might be able to knock someone out by throwing the brick at him before he could kill Jim Luke, or at least knock the lantern off the table so he could run.

The leader of the Klan was speaking when I raised up. "Rise," he said to the men at the table, and they rose and faced the two tall men standing at the door with Jim Luke. My heart went thump, and I saw Jim Luke jump about a foot when the leader said, "Now the secret password." Before anything else could be said, I took a running leap backward and swung my throwing arm, sending the brick through the window. There was a crash and the room went dark. I heard the door crash open and a white figure flew around the corner of the house hissing, "Run, run," and I needed no further urging.

In back of us I heard a trap snap and fierce cussing. Later from some place far behind us a few cars started up and it flashed through my mind to wonder where the Klan had hidden them, because when me and Jim Luke were waiting at the old Turner place we hadn't seen any lights or heard any car motors. Then I quit thinking of anything except keeping my feet going. Jim Luke peeled the sheet off of him and threw it into the bushes while still running. It took a while for it to sink in that if they were driving cars and we were running through the woods, they couldn't come after us, so we laid on the ground, taking deep breaths, and finally my breathing grew quiet.

I turned to say something to Jim Luke and he was

laying stiff, his eyes were bugged out and he was barely breathing. I yelled and started shaking him. "What's wrong? Are you shot, Jim Luke? What's the matter, talk, Jim Luke, please!" I yelled.

"Oh shut up, Sammy, and get off me," he said. "Sammy, do you remember when Pa said we could use the traps last winter?"

"Yes," I answered.

"Well, you remember we had a fight over who got the rusty ones and who got the shiny ones?" he asked.

"Yes," I said, and I knew the calmness of his voice wasn't calmness at all, but dead fear.

"Lord, Sammy! You remember Pa cut our names on a rusty one and a shiny one apiece?" he asked.

"Yes, Lord yes, Jim Luke, what are we gonna do?"

"Die!" Jim Luke snapped, and rose up slowly and started walking toward the house. I followed him even slower. The excitement had gone out of the killer's hunt. I didn't even want the money any more. Lord, I just wanted me and Jim Luke to live.

After a while Jim Luke waited for me to catch up with him. Then he put his arm around my shoulder. There were a lot of things I would have liked to have told him before I died, but I sort of squeezed him and he squeezed back, so I knew I didn't have to say anything, and that he liked me too. We weren't even quiet when we went through the window of our room. It seemed that nothing mattered.

Fear felt out of place in our familiar room, and we laid stiff on top of the covers, not even caring that Grandma would skin us for messing up the spread. We just lay holding hands, waiting for the Klan to come and get us. But our tired bodies betrayed our minds and we slept. Our fear was real and so was the danger, because the righters of wrong always shut up anybody who might betray their lowdown sneaking meanness. Just before sunup our barn burned, and old Ned, our beloved mule, with it.

CHAPTER 13

I awoke to a room full of red haze and the tormented screams of the damned in my ears. Jim Luke's freckles stood out black through the red haze, and he was shaking and hugging me at the same time saying in a hoarse voice, "They got us, Sammy, they got us."

Then Grandma was in the room yelling, "The barn! The barn! Go help Pa! Run!"

I don't know how long she yelled before we realized what she wanted. We broke for the barn, but when we got there Grandpa was standing, staring grimly at what was left. Then old Ned gave a last, weak scream and there was silence, except for the crackling of flames and the crashing of burned rafters as they fell. The smell of old Ned cooking made us gag.

"Gone, gone, gone," Grandpa muttered weakly, leaning against the rail fence that had surrounded the barn. Me and Jim Luke went and put our hands on Grandpa's shoulders, not saying anything, but we knew what he meant and felt guilty as hell.

We were feeling that we should have told him about the Klan, but didn't dare to do so now because he would have oiled his gun and gone hunting for them. And we knew what he meant when he muttered, "gone." It wasn't just old Ned, which was the worst part, but all of our summer work, our crops which were to keep us until planting time again, hay, corn, potatoes, onions, pumpkins, they had all been stored in the barn. When puffs of wind blew ashes that the barn had now become, it blew the smell of burned feathers also, for the chicken house had been built on the barn, so Grandma's chickens were gone too, along with the plows, harness and wagon.

When Grandma called us to come and put something in our bellies we went, but me and Jim Luke walked every bit as tired and old as Grandpa because we had all the guilt riding us.

Grandpa didn't say a word when Jim Luke poured him and me a cup of coffee. Grandma and Grandpa both were white and tired and sort of hopeless looking. Me and Jim Luke drank our coffee and left them talking about what in the world we were going to do through the winter.

Jim Luke closed the door to our room and stood leaning against it. He looked plumb wild. "Sammy," he said, "we gotta leave this place now."

"Jim Luke, we can't leave Grandpa like this now," I said, surprised that he had even thought of such a thing.

"That's just it, Sammy," he went on, "we gotta leave now afore they get in a worse fix or get hurt, 'cause the Klan is goin' to keep on 'til they get us. That barn was just a warnin', sayin' they's after us. Iffen we leave Ma and Pa a note sayin' we're goin' off to work to help build a new barn, Pa will tell the people about it and the Klan will think we left, but will know Ma and Pa know nothin' about all this. We'll say we'll be back by the time school starts. That way they'll nigh take the hides off'n us when we get back, but won't worry."

"You're right, Jim Luke, but where are we gonna go?" I asked.

"We'll hide in the woods," he said.

"How are we gonna eat?"

"We'll just have to eat what we can find, kill or steal 'cause we can't take nothin' from here, Ma and Pa might need it since the rest of the stuff burned. Sammy, you get some matches and take two blankets off the bed while I write the note," he said, as he hunted for a pencil, "and Sammy, we're gonna get them dad-blamed bas- tards or die tryin'."

"Okay, Jim Luke, I'll help you all I can, but what about Raven Megan and Doc?" I asked.

"Well, we can't go nigh them now," he said, " 'cause we're pizen to anybody the Klan might see with us, and the sons-o-bitchin' low-down dogs, if they would quit hiding like the curs they are, behind sheets and in gangs, we might have a lot better chance to find them. And I'll tell you this, Sammy, I ain't got no pity for any of them dogs now. Now you get a move on, we got to get out of here. Hurry!" he snapped, and I did.

I wrapped the matches in some paper and took an ex- tra box of salt Grandma had and rolled everything in two blankets from our bed. I made sure we had our pocketknives and hatchet. Jim Luke put the note in the middle of the bed with a pin, and we slid out through the window for the last time for a week. Of course, we knew we would have to be back before school started, if the good Lord saw fit to let us live that long.

"You know, Jim Luke," I said as we cut through the orchard, "I feel bad about not letting Raven Megan and Doc know where we're goin'."

"I do too, Sammy John," he answered, "but I think it's best this way, leastways iffen we get killed it'll only be us."

"Where we goin', Jim Luke? I mean we have to have a place to sleep," I said.

"Well, Sammy, the place less likely they will come lookin for us is the old Turner place. They'd never think to look back there for us," he answered. After thinking it over for a spell I knew he was right. "Let's go, Sam- my," he said, "and try to pick up some food, my belly's gettin' mighty nigh empty. Sam and Mable Jackson allus has fruit trees and a big garden, maybe they ain't picked everythin' yet."

"But anyhow, Jim Luke," I said, "I wish we'd brought the dogs. They could have tree'd somethin' or caught a rabbit."

"I know, Sammy," Jim Luke replied, "but they would've given us away. Everybody knows our dogs. And Sammy, from now on don't talk no more than you can help, and allus stay hid as much as you can. We gotta be quiet and sneakin', or at least try. Just follow me and don't talk till I say so."

With that Jim Luke slipped off the trail and we slid through the trees like shadows. At first I was tired, then I started imagining that we were Indian warriors out scouting for a war party. I hissed at Jim Luke and told him what we were. He nodded. Most of the time he acted like he was too old to pretend, but when he did join me he went all out. So we tried to walk without bending grass or breaking twigs. Sometimes we wiggled for a way on our bellies.

When we got to the Jackson place on the wooded side, we lay flat behind a log with just our eyes peeking over the top. To attack or not was the question. The answer was not for a while because we saw big Mable Jackson come out and stop to pull sweet potatoes out of the garden. She weighed as near four hundred pounds as she did to three hundred, and Jim Luke poked me, whispering, still pretending to be a warrior.

"Heap big squaw, bigger'n hell," he said.

I sniggered and said, "Iffen we just had the hide off'n her hind end, we could make tepee for whole Indian village."

"Uhumm, Little Fox speak with true tongue. If pale face husband had cows with hind ends like squaw, white man make much wampum," he said.

I burst out laughing and Jim Luke pushed my head down into rotting bark and musk from the log and laid on me. About when I was sure I would smother to death he let me up and whispered, "Warrior steal pale face food."

I peeked over the log. Mabel Jackson wasn't to be seen so we crawled under the barbed wire fence and I watched the back door while Jim Luke stuffed his overalls with sweet potatoes. Then he tied the legs at the bottom with string so they wouldn't fall out. I nearly burst out sniggering again because he looked so fat and lumpy with his britches full of sweet potatoes, and had to walk spraddle-legged and slow. We eased around the fence and on to the smokehouse. Nearly all people locked their smokehouse at night, but left them open in the daytime. Jim Luke eased the door open. We could hear big Mable rattling pots and pans while I slipped through the door. Bacon and hams hung from the rafters. Lord, I'd never seen so much meat. No wonder Mable was fat. With Jim Luke whispering to hurry, I cut down part of a side of bacon with my pocketknife and looked hungrily at the hams. But they were too big to carry, so I grabbed two jars of peaches from the shelf and we went on as fast as we could to the log where we had left our blankets.

Deep in the woods, long before we got to the Turner place, we built a smokeless fire. While sweet potatoes baked on the top ashes, we toasted bacon on sharp sticks. Then we ate the peaches with our fingers and drank the juice, saving the squashy potatoes for last. It was close to sundown when we finished stuffing ourselves. We rolled the leftover potatoes, bacon and even the leftover fruit jars in our blankets and headed for our temporary home.

By the time we were settled down in the rickety Turner house it was good dark. The lamp glass had broken, and our blankets lay in a corner. The fall nights were getting cool, but we didn't dare build a fire in the fireplace for fear somebody would see it. It was too early to sleep and too dark to do anything else, so we rolled up close to each other in our blankets and talked.

"Jim Luke, you think the K.K.K. is really gonna get us?" I asked, and moved closer to him. " 'Cause, Jim Luke, I don't really want to die, in fact I'm sorta scared to. You reckon we oughta pray?"

"Well, it sure wouldn't hurt none, Sammy," he said,

and put part of his blanket over me. "I don't want to die neither. They's a lot of things I wanted to do afore I went, but Sammy, if we gotta go, let's pray we go brave as we can."

"But Jim Luke," I said, "I don't feel brave, I just feel like kickin' and screamin' and a yellin', 'I don't want to go!' "

"I know, Sammy, I don't reckon most people want to go," he said, "but when it's their time there ain't much use carryin' on about it."

"But Jim Luke," I said, "it really ain't fair, I mean it makes me mad 'cause them buggers they ain't got no right to say for a person to die or live."

"You're damn right, Sammy, and it's up to us to see they get caught. Iffen we can afore they get us," he said.

"But, Jim Luke, they is all over the South. Why does grownups let them get away with it? I really do wonder."

"Well, mostly Sammy" he said, "real folks can't really believe other grown-up men would gang up and do such things. And besides, just one at a time they are cowards, it takes a bunch to have any bravery, or what they call courage, and then they have to have all the odds."

"Well, I hate them, Jim Luke," I said, "I just hate them for a wantin' to get rid of us."

I felt it was just so unfair I wanted to cry, but Jim Luke put his arm around me and said, "Don't worry, Sammy, maybe we'll get out, or we'll sure die trying'. I feel sorry for Ma and Pa, maybe we ought to a told them, but it seemed better at the time not to. Now you try to sleep because we've got to wake up pretty soon and go spyin', and Lord I hope we catch one."

"Maybe we could capture him and make him tell, but Jim Luke, all we got's our pocketknives and we can't very well skin anyone."

"Well," he said, "I still got the pistol you found in the pond, but I ain't got no shells. Maybe we could bluff them."

"I sure hope so, Jim Luke, I sure hope so," I murmured sleepily as Jim Luke's arm tightened around me. I slept thinking that old "Shoot fire" Jim Luke was the best, bravest person I ever did see.

CHAPTER 14

I didn't feel like I liked him so much when he shook me awake before I hardly got my eyes closed good. He felt around for some sweet potatoes in the dark and gave me one. We wiped off all the dirt we could on our britches and ate them raw. They were cold and sweet and sort of woke a body's mouth up. The frost on the ground did the same for my feet when we stepped outside. Even Jim Luke jumped around stomping to get warm blood to his feet.

"Jim Luke," I said, "who in the world we gonna spy on this time of the night?" I felt like complaining.

"Well," he said, "I changed my mind. We're gonna go to see Doc and Raven Megan and talk it over with them. And on the way we're gonna spy on the Jacksons since we're passin' there anyhow. So come on and be quiet. From now on we gotta do our sleepin' days and our livin' nights." I didn't argue, I just followed him. I was so glad we were going to see Raven Megan and Doc. I would have swum an icy creek, buck naked, and not said a word.

We knew the way out to the Jackson house because we had been visiting there with Grandma and Grandpa. When we got there the house was dark, but Jim Luke led the way on his hands and knees, around the house and under the bedroom window. We could hear Sam talking before we got there, and we hunkered down under the window. The words were plain; almost too plain.

Sam was saying, "Mable, why in the cat hair won't you give me some?"

She sounded real cross when she said, " 'Cause I been workin' hard, Sam Jackson, and I'm tired and want to sleep, and you shut your mouth before you wake up the young'ns."

"Aw, come on, Mable, I just need a little," Sam sort of whined.

"Oh hush up! You allus got to get jist a little, Sam Jackson." Mable really sounded mad now.

Me and Jim Luke almost jumped from our skins when Sam suddenly yelled, "Well, there was a time when you didn't complain, you big heifer. Remember behind the big oak by the creek afore we wed?"

Before we could hear her answer, Jim Luke grabbed my hand and dragged me around the house. We hit the trail on the other side and walked fast. I didn't say anything and neither did Jim Luke. In fact, I felt sort of ashamed that we had listened for so long, and reckoned it would be hard to look at Sam Jackson in the eye if we ever lived to meet again.

There wasn't any light at Doc's place either, but one came on when Jim Luke pounded on the door. "Who's there?" Doc called, sounding grumpy with sleep.

"Jim Luke and Sammy John," Jim Luke called back.

In no time flat Doc pulled the door open and had us inside. The couch was all tumbly with a blanket on it, and Raven Megan came yawning through the bedroom door.

"Where the hell you boys been?" asked Doc, sharp like. "Your pa's been tryin' to find you, Jim Luke."

"Are you gentlemen hungry?" asked Raven Megan.

I nodded yes, and Jim Luke answered Doc, "Doc, we had to hide out. Did Pa tell you about our barn burnin'?"

"Yes, but what has that got to do with it?"

"It was the Klan," said Jim Luke, and he told Doc about the traps and what we had been doing. Only he left out what we had heard at the Jacksons' a little while before.

Raven Megan said we looked hungry, and made us sit down at the kitchen table. She gave us soup she had heated from a can, and a glass of milk. Doc looked mad, but talked softly to us, like it was somebody else he was mad at.

After we had eaten, Jim Luke pushed his chair back and said, "Doc, we came to ask you what you think maybe we ought to do. If we go home the Klan will kill us 'cause they know by now we found the body. But they don't know you and Raven Megan know. Lord, we ain't got many neighbors left to spy on, and so far our spying ain't done much good. 'Sides, Sammy John don't want to die."

He ran out of breath, and when he stopped to get it I jumped in with, "And Jim Luke don't want to die neither." He glared at me but I kept on, " 'Sides, we can't go home 'cause they would hurt Grandma and Grandpa. And Doc, iffen there ain't no reward money or iffen we can't find the killer, we're gonna die anyhow from starvin', 'cause they burnt all our winter food in the barn. When the F.B.I. man gets here he won't be able to find the Klan members neither, 'cause they sneak around all wrapped up in sheets."

Then I, too, ran out of breath, but before Jim Luke could say anything Doc said, "Well, thanks to you boys he will have one good clue, because I sewed up Jim Baker's leg that looked like a bunch of wolves had chewed it. Your trap worked, boys."

"Jim Baker!" Me and Jim Luke nearly screamed at the same time. Lord, we'd known Jim all our lives. He lived with his ma on the other side of our south pasture, and he was a mean one. Once there had been whispers that he had raped Rosey Jean Tuttle when she was about fourteen, but me and Jim Luke didn't ask any questions about it because Grandma would have slapped our heads off for that kind of talking. But all the same, Rosey did have a young one, and took it every place with her plain to see, and I determined to take a good look at it the next chance I could, to see if I could see Jim in it.

"What can we do, Doc?" Jim Luke burst in.

"Well, boys," he answered, "the only thing I can see is to lay low until the F.B.I. man gets here. I could try to get you and Raven Megan out of the state, but I really doubt if we could make it because if the Klan has members on the sheriff's side they would be alerted and we wouldn't get far. This is the damnedest thing I have ever run into."

"If we lay low around here, when the F.B.I. man comes, if they can make Jim Baker talk, maybe they will be able to find out . . . ," and my voice trailed off.

I was staring straight across the table from Jim Luke while Doc talked. I heard the sound of glass breaking and saw Jim Luke's hair part directly down the middle before the shot sounded in my ears. Doc grabbed Raven Megan and threw her down on the floor, laying over her, yelling, "Get down! Get down!," but I was too busy staring at Jim Luke because his green eyes sort of crossed and blood started dripping from the part in his hair. His face went pale and he swallowed a few times, and very weakly he said, "Shoot fire," and sort of surprised like he slumped off his chair on to the floor.

I stood and stared at him laying there a little longer before losing my senses and screaming, "Doc, they killed Jim Luke! Jim Luke's been shot! The bastards have done killed old shoot fire Jim Luke!" Then I didn't remember any more for a while.

CHAPTER 15

When I came to, I was laying on the couch with Raven Megan slapping me and saying, "Sammy, oh Sammy," over and over. When I tried to raise up, she pushed me back down.

"Jim Luke! Jim Luke!" I called.

"Shh, he's all right, Sammy, he's all right," she said. "Jim Luke's just fine, he's just sleeping."

"Jim Luke's sleeping now, and he's just fine," Doc spoke up from the foot of the couch, "the bullet just grazed his head a little. But listen, Sammy, you have to get away from here."

"Hey, Doc," I said, fully awake now, "is them men that shot Jim Luke still outside?"

"No," he told me, "I think it was only one man and he ran off when you started yelling that Jim Luke had been killed. But we better get out of here before he comes back with more men. We want you to lead us to the old Turner place. I don't think they will come back there after the traps you and Jim Luke set for them. Do you think you can lead us there?"

"Yes," I said, "it would be closer to go by Rudy Spraddle's place, but they might see us," I told him.

"Don't worry about that, Sammy," Doc said, "Rudy and his bunch have moved bag and baggage without a word to anyone. I went by their house yesterday to see how the new baby was doing and the whole place has been cleaned out." I snickered a little and wished Jim

Luke was awake to hear that we had done some good.

"But, Doc," I said, getting a new idea, "iffen you leave, they will search this place and find the dead man."

"Don't worry about that," Doc laughed, "where he's at they won't find him."

"Well, what if the F.B.I. man comes while you're gone?" I asked.

"Don't worry about that either, Sammy, I'll be back by that time. It's you boys and Raven Megan I want to get out of danger. Now come, you carry my medicine bag for I have to carry Jim Luke. Raven Megan will have to carry blankets and some food. I wish we could take my pickup, but the lights could be seen for miles. Raven, have you got the flashlight?"

"Yes, Jason," she said, looking sort of pale. That Raven Megan was the bravest girl I had ever heard tell of.

I went and took Doc's bag off the table, and Raven Megan picked up a huge sack and took some blankets off the couch. Doc came from the bedroom carrying Jim Luke all wrapped up in a blanket, with just his head showing through. He had a white bandage around it, and he didn't wake up. Boy would he be surprised to wake up in the old Turner house. Doc looked all around, then blew out the lamp. With him and Raven Megan following, we took to the woods.

I felt good because almost always Jim Luke had got to lead. By the time we got to the Spraddle place, I felt like my arms had been pulled from their sockets by Doc's bag, and Raven Megan was staggering under her heavy load.

"We will rest at the creek," I kept telling her, "it's just a little ways."

But when we got there Doc wouldn't let us sit long. He said, "It's getting light in the east and I wanted to have you people under cover by daybreak."

We went across the foot bridge and kept to the trees by the fields. Even Doc was breathing hard and shifting

110

Jim Luke around for a better hold. The air had turned cold and the frost covered the ground like ice. I had to keep dancing around to keep my feet from getting numb.

Raven Megan kept gasping out, "I'm going to get you some shoes, Sammy, if it's the last thing I ever do! You hear that, Jason? If something happens to me, I want Sammy and Jim Luke to have new shoes."

Doc didn't waste his breath, he just sort of nodded and smiled.

The sun was peeking red over the ridge when we crossed over the last open field to the old Turner house.

Raven Megan slumped down on the doorstep, letting her load fall to the ground. I pushed open the door and set Doc's bag on the table and showed him our blankets in the corner. He laid Jim Luke on them, felt his wrist, and said something about the constitution of a horse, then covered him up.

I slumped down beside him while Doc carried in Raven Megan's bundles. She staggered in behind him. He set the food on the table, took a pistol out of his pocket and laid it there too. Then he spread blankets close to me and Jim Luke for Raven Megan to lay on.

When she lay down, he bent over and he kissed her. He jumped about a foot when I said, "Doc, I been meanin' to ask you iffen you will marry Raven Megan so she can stay around here? Me and Jim Luke would, but Grandma wouldn't let us."

Raven Megan started giggling and Doc laughed. "Well, Sammy," he said, "I have been wanting to ask the lady, and I couldn't have put it better myself."

I kept waiting for Raven Megan to say yes, but they just kept staring at each other and kissing, so I rolled over close to Jim Luke to get warm and went to sleep.

When I woke up Jim Luke was sitting at the table eating some sandwiches Raven Megan was making. Doc wasn't to be seen. When Raven Megan saw me sitting up, rubbing the sleep from my eyes, she said, "Come and eat before it gets dark."

I hurried up to the table and said, "Hey, Jim Luke, you know what happened to you?"

"Yeah. Raven Megan told me. Reckon it's a good thing they hit my head, iffen it had been any place else it woulda killed me," Jim Luke answered, laughing, and me and Raven Megan laughed too.

"Where's Doc?" I asked her.

"He went to scout around his house to see if anyone has been there. He'll be back before long. Here, you'd better eat," she said, handing me a sandwich of cold roast beef. "We need some water, gentlemen," she said, "but I don't know what to put it in. Is there a spring or something or will we have to go to the creek?" She asked us.

"There's a spring down nigh the woods. Iffen you could empty them soup cans, me and Sammy John could go and get them full after dark," Jim Luke said.

"But what could I do with the soup?" Raven Megan asked.

"Well, I reckon I could eat that chicken noodle even if it is cold, 'cause being' shot makes a feller's belly nigh empty. I reckon Sammy could eat a canful too." Raven Megan laughed and opened the soup, then she gave us each a can. It tasted kind of greasy, but had a good chicken flavor.

Dirt kept sifting down from the roof. The room was the only whole one left in the house, and it was rotten in places. The only furniture was the table and two rickety chairs.

Doc came in about the time we finished eating, and me and Jim Luke got up so him and Raven Megan could sit down. Doc looked tired and didn't say much while he was eating, then he changed the bandage on Jim Luke's head.

When he finished he said, "Now listen, all of you, I am dead tired and have to get some sleep. I hid some pans, some more food and some sheets by the oak near the creek bank. When it's dark, you boys go and get them, but be sure to hurry, and be sure to hunt the ground all the way there and back."

He spread some blankets out and started to lay down. He took one boot off and had the other one about off when he stopped and looked up at us. Then he said, "The hills are alive with your kinfolks looking for you, and the men of the Klan are doing the same thing. It's confusing because we don't know who belongs to the Klan, so we can't trust anyone."

He finished taking his boot off and sat there with his elbows on his knees. He reached up and got hold of Raven Megan's hand and pulled her over closer to him.

"Now, Raven Megan," he said, "I have been thinking, and I want to ask you a question, and no matter how you hate to do it, answer it anyway. Listen, you made someone mad that belonged to the Klan and that's why they burned the cross on your yard. Now, who pawed you?" he asked softly.

Raven Megan's face went red and she glanced at me and Jim Luke, then back to Doc, and he said, "You have to answer, Raven Megan, our lives might depend on it."

"Well, it . . . it . . ." she stuttered, "well, it was the boys' Uncle Shall. He pretended to bring me wood, but really he just kept trying to put his hands all over me, so I slapped him hard and said I would tell his wife."

"But you told us he was just bringin' you wood!" Jim Luke burst in.

"I know, Jim Luke, and I am sorry. I just didn't want you to feel bad," she said sad like.

"But, Jim Luke," I said, "remember how the Klan talked under the rotten tree that night, saying how Uncle Shall didn't belong?"

"Wait a minute, Sammy," Doc said, "remember the members aren't supposed to know each other. Of course, they do a lot of times, or have a good idea, but not one of them know the leader or the Grand Wizard. And I'm sorry, Jim Luke, but you see your Uncle Shall's fingerprints were on the dead man's belt buckle I sent to the F.B.I."

I felt so weak and drained, and Jim Luke was white-looking and protested, "But Doc, he's my kin, my brother-in-law, and 'sides, our barn burned. Surely to the world he wouldn't order his wife's folks food burned."

"I know it seems bad, Jim Luke, but most people will do anything if they believe it's right, especially fanatics like the Klan,"Doc said.

"Listen," I said excitedly, "remember, Jim Luke, the leader was taller than Uncle Shall."

Then Doc put in with, "Yes, but Sammy, the hoods of the costumes make the men look much taller. Boys, I'm sorry as hell, but he was the only one that Raven Megan had trouble with, and it stands to reason that he had something to do with it."

"But surely to God he wouldn't kill us, his own kin," Jim Luke kept protesting, but I could tell he was beginning to believe it, and so was I. I felt sick and ashamed. So did Jim Luke. So Doc said him and Raven Megan would go outside for a minute. Me and Jim Luke felt so ashamed for Uncle Shall that we didn't want to look at them right then.

We were both remembering the fishing trips and how Uncle Shall always teased us about girls, or we thought he was teasing.

I remember once when Grandpa wasn't along he said, "Boys, I sure have a nice-looking little blonde, the purti-est little blonde you ever did see." I remember it sort of shamed us because we knew Aunt Imie was dark head-ed, and Jim Luke changed the subject fast.

Finally, Jim Luke looked at me with a sickly grin. "Well, Sammy, if Uncle Shall is the Grand Wizard, it musta really scared the pee outa him when we burned the cross on his yard."

"Man, I reckon," I grinned back, "but, Jim Luke, I just plain don't know what to do about him."

"I don't neither, Sammy, but it's for sure we can't let the bastard kill us just 'cause he's kinfolk. I sure the hell ain't that noble, 'cause one shot in the noggin is enough for this old cat."

"I'd just soon not to have one," I said, "and, boy, that old Uncle Shall must really be dirt to burn our barn and old Ned." Thinking about old Ned filled me with hate toward Uncle Shall, and Jim Luke's face slowly turned grim.

Looking at him, I knew Uncle Shall was in for it. The memory of old Ned screaming and the picture of Uncle Shall pawing Raven Megan suddenly wiped out memories of fishing trips. Kin or no kin, I was as ready as Jim Luke to set the law on him. We just sat silently, thinking and waiting for Doc and Raven Megan to come back. I think we both grew up a little.

When Doc and Raven Megan came back in, it was almost dusky dark. Doc said as far as he could tell there weren't any signs of anyone around, so me and Jim Luke slid out the door and ran for the timber. We found the stuff Doc had left and came back by the spring, slowly and carefully. We filled the cans with water, and after we had drunk all we wanted, we filled the cans for Raven Megan.

Stars were peeping out all over the sky, and I had a sudden longing for Grandpa and Grandma. It seemed that all the living me and Jim Luke did any more was at night.

It was a lot darker in the cabin, and we couldn't see Doc and Raven Megan until our eyes got used to it. Doc was sleeping, and she whispered that we were supposed to wake him in an hour, that he was going back to hide and wait for the F.B.I. man. She told us that Doc's phone lines had been cut, so there was no way to hurry the man up.

Jim Luke whispered to me that we ought to go spy on Uncle Shall since he was the center of all our trouble in the first place. He wanted to make sure the bastard hadn't hurt Aunt Imie. It seemed such a shame that his very own sister had married such a no-good dog, and we both felt sorrowful about the little young ones they had.

Raven Megan eased over and asked what we were whispering about. We told her that we were going to spy on Uncle Shall, and for her not to leave the cabin whatever she did. In fact, we told her she ought to climb into the loft and take all signs of our being there with her. We said we would whistle three times before we came in when we got back, and for her to tell Doc to do the same. She begged us not to go, and finally burst into tears and said she would tell Doc. Jim Luke told her it was our duty to turn in Uncle Shall and to spy on him ourselves since he was our kin. But it was no use telling her, she just kept saying, "No, no, you mustn't, it's dangerous." So we just quit arguing and ran out of the door before she could wake Doc.

CHAPTER 16

The dark closed around us and our familiar homeland had become a cruel cold place where kin killed kin, and men we thought we knew sneaked around in sheets doing deeds of madness and evil. For no reason I knew I was silently weeping for a redheaded man who would never get to see the sun or eat potatoes any more. I wept for my fat, snuff-dipping Aunt Imie who would have to live with us and raise her young ones, and Uncle Shall who wouldn't get to go fishing and laugh about women he was stuck on. Mostly I was crying that he wouldn't kill us first.

My toes were so cold with frost they hurt, and I didn't know I was making any noise until Jim Luke said soft like, "Quit a snifflin', Sammy, we'll get them all right, leastways I hope to God we do. I feel like bawling myself, but once I start I do it so loud and so long I would lead the whole country to us. So be quiet, Sammy, we'll cry later, after we be safe. And, Sammy, usually good times come after bad, so sometime when they do we'll forget this. Now come on, and quiet like. Reckon we'll have to go on our bellies most of the way since Doc said the country was alive with men a lookin' for us."

I truly doubted if any good times would ever come again, but I hushed, and when Jim Luke froze in his tracks I did too. We heard voices coming along the path by the creek. We dropped to our bellies and lay quiet as

117

the dead, and silently thanked God that the men were going the other way from the cabin that hid Raven Megan and Doc.

The men carried a lantern, and we recognized Herb Jeffries and Luther Thompson, but didn't dare call to them because we were more or less between the devil and the deep blue sea, not knowing who was hunting us for Grandpa or who was hunting us for the Klan. So we just didn't say anything, but soon as they were out of sight we waded the creek, afraid to take the bridge in case somebody was watching it. Jim Luke knew where to cross over the shallow part. Still, it wet us to our knees and we had to do some fast jumping up and down on the other side to get the blood going again in our frozen feet.

The night was dark, for one of the Southern storms was rolling up. The thunder was faint, but jagged streaks of lightning ripped the clouds apart. Now and then a light breeze blew leaves from the trees, and when our bare feet hit them they seemed to crash with noise. Suddenly the whole woods seemed alive with noise. By the time we had crawled and crept to the hill that led up to Uncle Shall's, the breeze had risen and the trees looked like bowing giants. It was like being covered with fresh blood and moving through a jungle full of hungry, evil creatures.

Jim Luke whispered as we started up the hill, "Whatever you do, Sammy, hang onto me, and when the storm breaks dig in the ground and hang on." I told him okay, but I had been in enough storms to know what to do. By now the world looked green from the constant lightning, and the thunder was loud enough to shake the hills. Now and then there was a sharp, heavy crash and the smell of brimstone filled the air where a tree had been struck. We knew better than to get under a tree during a storm, but were afraid to stay in the open. If it hadn't been for the lightning lighting our way, we would have been hopelessly lost in black darkness.

We kept to the line of trees, but when a huge tree was
118

struck just behind us, Jim Luke grabbed my head in both of his hands and yelled in my ear, "Run for the barn, Sammy," and we did. Blowing leaves mixed with hailstones hit our faces, pounding upon us as we ran. We ran under brush and scraped our toes on rocks, then straightened our course again by the light from the lightning flashes.

I lost Jim Luke once, but when lightning flashed again he found me and grabbed my hand and pulled me with him. We flew past Uncle Shall's house and straight for the barn lot. The storm was hitting hard, and I doubt if he would have heard a herd of elephants above it. It took a while for us to pull a stall door open against the wind, and when we had it open and were inside, the wind slammed it with a sound like a shot. We went up the ladder to the hayloft and buried ourselves in the warm, dry hay.

We couldn't talk for hail made a loud drumming noise on the tin roof of the barn. The warmth of the hay seeped through me, even my feet were beginning to get warm. After a while the hail gave way to a downpouring rain, and we could faintly see the cow in the stall below. We knew every part of the barn as well as we did our own, because we had done Uncle Shall's chores to get him to take us fishing.

What a shame that he had to turn out meaner than a skunk and to be the Grand Wizard. He had killed a man, and I wondered how many other crimes he had gotten away with. Come to think of it, the square set of his body had a mean look to it, especially his small, mean, gray eyes.

I heard Jim Luke squirming around in the hay to get more comfortable. A little later thunder crashed right over us. It must have opened up the sky, because rain poured down harder than ever. Warmth crept over me and the hay smelled all sunshiny. Everything faded, and my tired body gave up. I slept and I didn't even dream.

For a while after we woke, we were wild eyed and lost, not knowing where we were. Bright sun shone through the cracks of the barn loft, and Jim Luke was spitting and coughing hay dust out of his throat. By the time he got it cleared, I remembered well enough why we were here.

"Sammy, we gotta get out of here," he croaked, but then it was too late because we could hear Uncle Shall calling the dogs to feed them, and we knew that before we could get out of the barn he would be there.

My mind went blank, and I whispered desperately, "What are we gonna do, Jim Luke? Lord, what are we gonna do?"

Jim Luke was looking around wild eyed, saying, "Hush, hush." My glance followed him. I could see no place to hide. There were just piles of hay we could burrow under. But he was liable to stab us with a pitchfork while throwing hay down to the cow. Jim Luke looked up and I did too. He didn't have to say a thing because the rafters had an old screen door and some gunny sacks across them, along with some old hoes, worn to just thin strips of metal. We heard Uncle Shall unlocking the barnyard gate.

Jim Luke gave me a boost and shinnied up after me. There was barely enough room for both of us, and we had to wrap around each other and hold our feet a little up in the air. We could hear Uncle Shall below us now, and soon he would climb the ladder and throw hay to the cows so he could milk while they ate. We only breathed enough to barely keep us living while the sound of Uncle Shall climbing the ladder came to our ears. I wish I could say here that we coolly and calmly captured Uncle Shall and turned him over to the F.B.I. man.

What really happened was that Jim Luke sort of tried to twist his head around to peek down at him and the screen door, with us on top, fell, right on top of Uncle Shall's head, knocking him back down the ladder. Before he could come to his senses, me and Jim Luke came untangled, and shedding straw like feathers, tore down the ladder past Uncle Shall, and were in the

120

woods before we even know if we had broken our necks, arms or legs. As we ran we could hear Uncle Shall yelling, "Come back here, you little bastards!" But we didn't stop until we waded across the creek. We had to stop in the last stand of trees across from the old Turner place because we didn't dare cross the open meadow to the house until dark.

We laid on our bellies, peering through the heavy underbrush, panting like dogs with our tongues hanging out. If Raven Megan and Doc were still there, there was no sign of them that I could see.

"Shoot fire, I'm hungry," Jim Luke said, as soon as we could get our wind.

"Well, I am too, but reckon we'll have a long wait 'til dark," I said.

"I don't know about that, Sammy, see how tall the grass is? We could crawl on our bellies slow, and it would be hard for a body to see us. 'Sides, a body ain't no deader starved than shot or hung." That made sense to me, so we started crawling.

Doc must have seen us, because just before we could whistle, and it seemed like we had been crawling forever, he opened the door and grabbed us in. He cussed some and Raven Megan started kissing us and yelling at us at the same time.

We shook them off and headed for the table, and came to a screeching halt because a strange man sat there. He was built small; not a lot bigger than Jim Luke. He wore store-bought clothes and a necktie. He had dark hair with gray in it and had blue eyes that looked like they were laughing.

"It's all right boys," Doc spoke up, "this is Mr. Roberts from the F.B.I. Now you fellows fill him in on what you were up to last night. Raven Megan and I have told him the rest."

Mr. Roberts gravely shook our hands saying he was glad to meet us, that we had done a good job and that the F.B.I. could use men like us. His voice was deep and at the same time soft. He made us feel proud.

While we ate some sandwiches Raven Megan made for us, Jim Luke told about going to spy on Uncle Shall, the storm, the door, and us falling on Uncle Shall. The grownups laughed, but our faces were pretty red, and Jim Luke said he reckoned we hadn't done so well. But Mr. Roberts insisted and Doc did too that we had done better than they could have.

Then Mr. Roberts questioned us about the body we had found, about Uncle Shall and what the countryside around here was like. He asked us about our neighbors, and Grandpa and Grandma, and we told him everything we could think of that had happened. Jim Luke said for him to remember that he could catch all the Klan he wanted, but we had to take care of Uncle Shall ourselves because he was our own kin. It was the hill code to take care of our own.

We sort of got the impression he went along with us without his saying anything, and he asked us if we would stay quietly hid in the house while he, Doc and Raven Megan went to take care of some things. We promised, and Doc and Raven Megan both hugged us. Mr. Roberts shook our hands again. We sat around and talked until it was good and dark, then the grown-ups left, promising to be back for us that night some time.

Me and Jim Luke ate up the rest of the food, slipped to the spring for a drink of water, then came back and rolled up in our blankets and relaxed for the first time that day. Once or twice I heard a noise in the loft but Jim Luke said it was mice, so I soon didn't pay any more attention to them.

"You know, Sammy," Jim Luke said, "I bet we won't be able to lay on our backsides or sit for a week after Pa gets through with us."

"I don't care, Jim Luke," I answered, "just as long as I know we be alive. I am sure gettin' tired of hiding, and man would some of Grandma's hot bread, beans and taters taste good now."

"I know how you feel, Sammy, and you know since I found out Uncle Shall's the leader of the Klan, even reward money don't seem good. I figure iffen we live to get any I'm gonna give my part to Aunt Imie to raise the young'ns on without letting her know where it came from."

"I reckon to do the same with my part, Jim Luke, but I was sure countin' on gettin' me a pair of danged boots, and I reckon I will have to figure out another way to make my ma feel sorry she married that city man afore comin' to get me," I said, sort of sad.

But I perked up when Jim Luke said, "I'm sorry about that, Sammy, but truth to tell I sure hated to see you leave and was a hopin' somethin' would happen so's you'd have to stay with me." It made me feel glad, and I scooted closer to him. I heard the stirring of the mice in the loft again, but soon forgot it.

"You know, Jim Luke, when my feet get cold I feel like I would give anythin' for a pair of shoes that would never wear out. But somehow it just don't seem right to make your own body comfortable by sellin' out another body. But that danged old Uncle Shall's a mean one, and iffen we don't he might hurt Aunt Imie or one of the young'ns sometime."

"I know it, Sammy, shhh, shh," Jim Luke stiffened and I did too, because I could see the white face of what looked like a ghost looking through the broken window. I wished it had been a ghost, but knew it was a member of the Klan. Before we could uncross our eyes, another face joined the first one and we were trapped, trapped like rats, and somebody outside was yelling, "Men, guard the window and doors." The voice was Uncle Shall's.

It was plain, even muffled under the sheet.

"Shoot fire! Shoot fire!" croaked Jim Luke, "we've been caught. Sammy, stand up and quit a shakin' and let's at least try to go brave." He rose to his feet and I did too, but had to hang onto him to keep from falling down again.

Suddenly, before we could move, the door burst open and the Klan members in their sheets and hoods filed through the open door. A lantern was lit and held high. Hands grabbed us and dragged us to the center of the room where the light fell on us good.

Everything settled down when a voice bellowed, "Quiet! The Grand Wizard will lead us in prayer before we settle this business before us."

Before praying could start, Jim Luke lost his head and I did too. If there was anything we didn't want to hear, it was Uncle Shall calling on the Lord to help him kill us.

Yelling, "Shoot fire," Jim Luke tore at Uncle Shall and I was close behind him. Hands grabbed me and held me tight, but Jim Luke jerked away and was climbing and kicking and pulling at the hood Uncle Shall wore. I stopped fighting the hand that held me, and I watched. Uncle Shall was pounding Jim Luke and his fist hit him across the mouth. Jim Luke started to bleed. The lick spun Jim Luke around, but yelling, "Shoot fire," he tore back at Uncle Shall.

This time he got a good hold on the hood, and as the other hands of the Klan members pulled at him, he pulled at the hood, and with a ripping sound it came open and off in Jim Luke's hands. Uncle Shall stood cussing and started kicking at Jim Luke. Then there were gasps of surprise as the Klan members saw their leader for the first time.

While the members were staring in their surprise, I pulled away from the hands that held me and ran to help Jim Luke, just in time to get a kick from Uncle Shall that sent me flying clear across the room. Jim Luke yelled, "Shoot fire," again, and tore into Uncle Shall. I saw Uncle Shall's hands clamp around his throat, then drop as the door burst open again.

Mr. Roberts and Doc came in with guns in their hands. Grandpa was with them and more men who looked like Mr. Roberts dropped from a hole in the loft near the fireplace.

Jim Luke came over to me and started puking, and one of his teeth came out. There was confusion with Jim

Luke throwing up and men cussing, and my head was going around where Uncle Shall had kicked me. I saw Doc come toward us, then the room rose up, spun around, and went dark.

CHAPTER 17

It was the day before school started. Me and Jim Luke were sitting on the high porch, favoring our hind ends where Grandpa's switch had nearly taken the hide off. The last warm sun of fall was sending beams of light bouncing off our new, black boots that we swung back and forth off the porch. We had slippers too. Raven Megan and Doc had bought them for us to wear to their wedding. We were going to be their best men.

There was a trial to go to too, where we were to be witnesses. Mr. Roberts said there was no doubt about the outcome of it. The way we understood it, the dead man had been a agitator, stirring up trouble. Doc told me and Jim Luke that he had come to talk to poor people so they would kick up a fuss about the way they had to live, and make the government help take care of them. So the Klan killed him so he wouldn't cause any trouble and find them out. Somehow it didn't make sense to me, because if a body was poor he ought to work and plant more, and the Klan ought not to sneak around killing folks that didn't see their way. Anyhow it seemed to me both sides ought to leave folks alone to live any way they wanted to.

The smell of frying potatoes and corn bread came out of the open window.

Aunt Imie was going to move in with us, and we were going to use her barn until our new one was built again. There wasn't any reward money, so we would all have

126

to work extra hard to feed all of us. There were a lot of things to do, what with the trial and the wedding. But best of all was the letter I had in my pocket from my ma.

Jim Luke's eyes laughed when I took it out and read it again for about the tenth time. It said she wanted me to come clear out to Colorado when school was out next summer just to see how I would like it. Best of all, if I wanted to I could bring Jim Luke with me, and if we wanted to, we could come home in the fall.

I put the letter back and started laughing. Jim Luke punched me in the ribs and I poked him back. We went tumbling off the porch, laughing fit to kill because we knew we were going to go. We were going to find out about that city man my ma had married, because we were good about finding out about folks. Mr. Roberts had said so. We'd soon find out if he was good for my ma.

Grandma called, "Come and eat while it's hot." We got up off the ground and dusted off our shiny boots. Old Pepper and Salt came tearing around the house. Everytime food was called they thought it meant them.

Me and Jim Luke laughed again, Yes sir! Me and that shoot-fire Jim Luke had a lot to do. For the first time since my ma left I didn't feel lonesome any more, and as we went through the door I said over again to myself, "Me and Jim Luke.